Jake

Melissa Stevens

TNT Publications

Copyright © 2025 by Melissa Stevens

All rights reserved.

No portion of this book may be reproduced in any form without written permission from the publisher or author, except as permitted by U.S. copyright law.

Dedication

This Demented Souls book, like all the Souls books, is dedicated to my dad, Wilmer 'Billy' Stephens.
When I started the series I used him as a major resource, as he'd been a police officer, machinist, gun smith, Harley rider, mechanic and so much more.
Now that he's gone, I write them in his memory.
Thanks Dad.
While I was growing up, my father had two of the best friends I've ever known of. They are the ones who taught me that family is more than just who you're related to. As I was working on *Maverick* we lost the last of them. Now that all three are gone, I miss the others nearly as much as I miss Dad.
From here on out, the Demented Souls books are dedicated to the men who taught me all about brothers by choice.
Frank Edwards (1950-2006)
Wilmer Stephens (Dad) (1952-2017)
George Claridge (1955-2022)

Contents

1	1
2	7
3	12
4	16
5	19
6	25
7	30
8	34
9	39
10	46
11	51
12	56
13	63
14	67

15	73
16	81
17	86
18	90
19	94
20	99
21	104
22	108
23	112
24	117
25	120
26	124
27	129
28	133
29	137
30	143
31	148
32	154
33	160
34	165

35	170
36	177
37	183
38	187
39	194
40	197
41	201
42	205
43	206
44	212
45	216
46	221
47	225
Epilogue	230

1

"Tell me again what the plan is?" Lurch asked Jake as Jake gave his bike one last inspection.

Jake fought the urge to sigh, as he explained the plan for today's ride for what felt like the fifteenth time, though he had to admit, this was probably only the second time he'd told the chapter president, and the first time had been weeks before. And he had to admit, if only to himself, that a lot had happened between now and then.

"We're going to Sturgis. Yes, we're weeks before the rally, but the guys from Tucson may not ever make it up for the rally, this is their chance to visit. It would be a shame to get this close and never make it to Sturgis."

"I got that part, that's not what I'm worried about." Lurch waved one hand dismissively.

Jake stopped what he was doing and looked over at Lurch. "What are you worried about? I didn't think there was anything to worry about with this trip."

"Tell me about this thing with the Kings." Lurch pinched the bridge of his nose as if Jake exhausted him.

"Cowboy wanted a chance to get together, pay his respects to Tuck before he leaves town. They'll meet us in Sturgis. They've got a big grill trailer that they'll haul down. They'll set it up at the park, people can come and go, grab food, see the town, chat, and have a little fun."

"Are you sure that's what they're after? Are you sure they're not harboring some kind of beef and trying to lure us out?"

Jake shook his head. "No chance. We're on good terms with them. Yes, there was a bit of a beef with them last year, but that was under their previous president. That incident triggered a coup. Cowboy's the new president and he's done everything he can to make sure we're on good terms. They help us and we help them, as far as that goes."

"We're taking our women. Are you sure it will be safe?"

"I'd say ninety-eight percent sure."

Lurch stared back at him. "Ninety-eight percent? Are you willing to risk Kerry's life on ninety-eight percent?"

Jake scowled. "I would. I'd risk my own mother's life on that same ninety-eight percent. We take bigger risks than that every day." He stood and faced the president of the chapter where Jake had decided to make his new home. "We get in a car, we get on a bike, we put our lives in not just our own hands, but the hands of every other person on the road, just by going from one place to another. We risk that everyone on the road is paying the same attention to traffic, or more, that we are. We risk that there won't be a robbery while we're in the gas station. We risk that we won't be victims of a drive by shooting or a car-jacking. Then there's the risk of developing an allergy or encountering what you have an allergy to. If you really think about it, you're risking death every time you eat, whether it's a snack or a meal or even just drinking your morning coffee."

Jake watched as Lurch slowly lifted one brow, but continued watching him without saying a word.

"What I'm saying is that if there's a risk to our women, then I'm confident it won't come from the Kings of Destruction. Their new leadership wants to be allies and is doing everything he can to that purpose. If it helps, they're bringing their women too."

"You could have led with that. It does help. While yes, most clubs aren't as protective of their women as we are, they don't typically bring them into trouble, at least not on purpose."

"Sorry. If I'd known it would make that much difference, I would have led with it. Any other concerns?"

"Nothing worth mentioning. Still planning to have us start the pre-ride meeting in an hour?" Lurch glanced toward the clearing they were using as the main camp, then back to Jake.

"That's the plan. I want to make sure there are no problems with my bike then I'll head over and be ready in case anyone has questions before the meeting."

"Sounds good. I'll see you there. I've got a couple of things to do before time to head out."

"See you." Jake went back to checking his bike, and when he'd finished, he made his way to the clearing, where he grabbed a soda from one of the coolers and went to one of the tables. He sat on the tabletop, propped one foot on the bench and cracked the seal on his soda. Everyone would start gathering soon, then he'd have to be ready to give people directions.

He couldn't wait to get on the road, there he would be able to relax, to lose himself in the ride, the wind in his face and the bike between his legs. Everything else would fade until it didn't matter. At least that was the plan.

They reached Sturgis with no problems, Jake let everyone know they'd be serving lunch at the park, where he'd let people know the plan for the afternoon and when food would be available, then had rounded up Talon and Steele and took them to find Miles.

"Where are you setting up the grill? I've got a couple of men to help with the cooking." He jerked one thumb over his shoulder to where the two prospects followed him.

"I've got a couple of men setting up the grill and the rest of the gear over there, on the edge of the lot. There are tables not far away people can use to eat, or they can wander off as they see fit. You been here before?" Miles asked.

"I haven't." Jake shook his head. "I haven't been up north very long, but I'm getting to know the area, slowly."

"Good. We usually come down a couple times a year, not always for the rally, but we try to make it at least once or twice a summer. It's a good place for meet ups, as people not from the area are usually up for a chance to see Sturgis, even in the off season."

"I totally get that. It's exactly why I chose it. We've got some visitors up from the charter chapter. I thought it would be an interesting visit for them, plus I hadn't made it here yet."

Miles nodded. "If you haven't been here yet, I can recommend a couple of places to visit if you'd like. I can make sure things get done here so we're ready to feed everyone."

"There are a couple of places I'd like to visit. The hall of fame and I've heard about some military museum in the area I'd like to check out."

"Into history?" Miles said with a grin. "That's cool. The Fort Meade Museum is neat if you're into that. I personally like the motorcycle museum better, but we all have our own thing." Miles shrugged.

"You sure you don't mind me disappearing for a while? I can hang around here and help make sure everything gets done." He looked around trying to find something that needed his attention but failing. Everything seemed to be taken care of, and without anyone directing each task. Jake couldn't help but be impressed. "You have this down to a science, don't you?"

"Not quite," Miles said with a laugh. "But I'm working on it. We go out a couple times a month, when the weather permits, so we've got it down pretty well. Did Cowboy find your president?" Miles' gaze scanned the area, as if looking for the two presidents.

"I introduced them when we arrived. Last I saw they were headed off that way together." He motioned toward the large oval track they'd seen on their way in. It had reminded him of the field from when he'd been in high school and in track and field. He'd wondered if it was part of the school grounds or just part of the park, but pushed the thought away as Miles asked him something. "I'm sorry. I didn't catch that, what was it again?"

"I asked which you plan on hitting first, the motorcycle museum or the military one."

"I'm not sure. Which one's closer?"

"The motorcycle museum, for sure. It's less than a mile that way," Miles pointed, "while Fort Meade is a couple miles in that direction." He indicated nearly the opposite direction.

"Good to know. That makes my decision." He checked his watch. "I've got what, two hours?"

Miles glanced at his own. "Sounds good. It's a little before we told everyone to be back for the meal, which will give you time to figure out enough to give directions to your people as they start showing up."

"Sounds good. One question though, and it's not critical, but it will make a difference on how my men handle mealtime."

"What?" Miles frowned.

"Who eats first, your men or your women?"

"Women and kids first. Then the men." Miles lifted one shoulder and let it fall. "It's how we've always done it." He lifted one brow. "Any problem with that?"

"Not at all. It's how we do it too, but if it went the other way, I'd need to warn the men first. They'd handle it, but by fixing plates and delivering them to their ladies before going back for their own."

"Oh. Good plan. I'll remember that for the next time we encounter a group that does things backwards." He shrugged again. "Not that we do a lot with other clubs. Especially after the crap with Tank last year, most of us don't trust the old connections. Cowboy and the rest of the leadership are checking through all our previous associations. We've cut ties in a couple places and in others," he used one hand to indicate where the members of the two clubs were mixing around them, "well, you can see we're making new connections."

"I was around for what went down between the Souls and the Kings with Ghost, but I wasn't in on any of it. I'm glad to hear you're re-evaluating the connections your old president made. Especially in light of what happened."

"We can talk more. It seems like we have more than a little in common, but it can wait. Go check out the museum. I've got everything here handled for a while, and if I have a problem, I've got your number. But I won't have a problem."

"Thanks." He slapped Miles on the back, then turned and went to his bike.

Less than five minutes later he was walking his bike back into a parking space in front of the museum. If he'd known how close it was, and his way around town, he might have walked. It would have been good to move a bit after a couple hours on the back of his bike to get to town.

2

Heather wandered through the museum her cousin had brought her to and wondered what the appeal was. Sure, she enjoyed it when Matt took her for a ride, like had today but whole museums to the history of the motorcycle? It just didn't do things for her. Though there were a couple of bikes she wouldn't mind a chance to get on, she knew there was a reason they were in the museum and not on the street. She knew there was no chance. Oddly one of them she kept finding herself standing in front of, staring at, was one that had a really long front end, at least compared to the others. The front tire was way out in front of the bike, and she couldn't figure out why.

There were a lot of things that stood out about the bike, which a sign on the other side of it called TheCanadabike. There was a whole list of unique things about it, most of which might as well be French to her. Not understanding her fascination, she turned and moved on, wondering how much longer her cousin would want to be here, and what the next stop was.

She still felt guilty that she was intruding on his trip like this, but he'd insisted he wouldn't have brought anyone else anyway and he didn't want to leave her at his place alone, just in case Mitch or any of the men he was indebted to figured out where she'd gone.

"Yo!" someone yelled somewhere else in the building, startling her. She jumped, then found herself searching the room, making sure no one had snuck up on her.

Heather couldn't help but shake her head when she realized what she was doing.

"There you are." Matt's head appeared around a corner. "You okay?" He frowned as he scanned her from head to toe and noticed the way her shoulders hunched forward, as if she was ready to be hit from behind.

"I'm good." She forced herself to smile, if only for his benefit. She hated being around so many strangers, not knowing who people were and who they knew. She'd been in North Dakota for a couple of weeks now and had gotten used to Matt's friends, or brothers as he called them, but now, they were hours away and meeting up with another club, she was afraid they knew the ones from Alabama, the ones Mitch was mixed up with. How could she be sure this new group wasn't going to try to take her back to him?

"This club has nothing to do with the one Mitch is mixed up with." Matt seemed to know what she was thinking.

Heather didn't know if it was because she was so transparent or because she'd been so worried about them finding her since she'd arrived. Either way, she couldn't stop the worry, so she just agreed with him.

"I know. You wouldn't do that to me. But what if you just don't know about their ties?" She couldn't help the tears that pooled in her eyes, but she blinked several times to keep them from falling and turned away so Matt wouldn't see them. He'd seen her break down far too often recently. She didn't want to add to that.

"You'll see soon enough." Her cousin didn't dismiss her fears. "But I'll be there with you, just in case, as will all the Kings. All you'll need to do is yell and one of us will come running. You know we'll all stand behind you."

"I know. And I appreciate it." Heather forced herself to take a deep breath and push away her worries. She was more than fifteen hundred miles from Mitch and his crew, there was no reason to think they would follow her this far. It wasn't like she'd taken anything of theirs or even that she knew anything of value. Only that she had been bartered to pay off a bet.

Heather didn't know how much money Mitch owed, and she didn't care either. She was not about to go with those men, men she didn't know and had no reason to trust. Given the fact that they'd let Mitch barter her body to pay off his debts made her trust them and him, even less.

"I know. I can't tell you how much I appreciate all the help you've given me."

Matt waved one hand in a dismissive gesture.

"No. I know you think it's nothing but it's not. It's a big deal to me. You've given me a place to go when I had nothing, a place to stay where I felt safe. A shoulder to cry on when it all got to be too much. You've helped me when no one else would."

His gaze flicked to something or someone behind her, then he nodded, as if he knew whoever it was, reminding her they were in public. She didn't need to air her problems, nor her insecurities to the world like this.

"I'll always be here for you, Heather, you know that. You're family."

"And I thank you for that." She gave him a quick hug then pulled away. "Take your time, I'm going to go wander through the gift shop and try to pull myself out of my funk."

"Okay." Matt smiled at her as she turned away, but caught her hand and pulled her back until her back hit his chest. "Remember what I told you," his voice was soft, "you're safe here." He kissed the top of her head, reminding her of the way he'd done exactly the same thing when she'd been six.

Heather nodded and forced herself to walk away. She knew her mood would only drag him down and make him worry about her. She didn't want to do that.

"Heather?" an unfamiliar voice called her name while she was wandering through the small gift shop, looking at things she wouldn't mind having, but wasn't willing to spend her meager cash on, and she would never ask Matt.

She looked up, half afraid of who might be calling her name, and hoping it was one of the Kings of Destruction and she just didn't recognize his voice for some reason. The face that greeted her was one of the last she expected to see.

"Aaron? What are you doing here? I haven't seen you in what? Ten? No, it's been longer than that. Twelve years?"

"It is you."

A smile spread across the face she hadn't seen since when? Junior year in high school. She and Aaron had been good friends, and she'd hoped for more, but he hadn't seemed interested, then his family had moved away, and she'd lost track of him. She'd never seen him again. Well, until now.

"What are you doing this far north? I didn't think you'd ever leave the coast."

The grin on Aaron's face made her want to move closer. Somehow, she knew there was no way he was involved with Mitch. They had never known each other. Mitch had moved to Mobile to go to University of Southern Alabama, even if she hadn't met him for several years. But that had been years after Aaron had left Alabama.

"I didn't plan to, but life happens." She lifted one shoulder and let it fall. "How have you been? Is this where your family settled?"

"I'm good. No, we went to California, then to Texas. Now my parents are in Florida, but I haven't been down to see them in a couple of years."

"How did you end up this far north, or are you just visiting?" She glanced around, hoping Matt wouldn't think Aaron was just some stranger bothering her.

"I moved up here almost a year ago. I live a couple hours away in Wyoming now. What about you?"

"I'm kind of in between places." She noticed for the first time he was wearing a leather vest like Matt wore. She didn't know why she hadn't noticed it before. "I'm staying with my cousin Matt for a while."

"Matt?" Aaron repeated, tilting his head back as his eyes rolled back in his head, as if he was looking for the information written inside his skull. "I don't know if I ever met him."

"I don't know that you did. He's several years older and didn't live in the area, so I didn't see him often."

She didn't say that when she had seen him, she'd been that annoying little cousin who wouldn't leave the older kids alone. Now she could see how clingy and irritating it must have been to the teenagers, but thankfully Matt had never made her feel unwanted.

"Heather?" The concern in Matt's voice made her smile.

"Looks like you'll meet him now though," she said to Aaron before turning to her cousin. "Hey. You'll never believe this. I ran into an old friend; one I haven't seen in at least ten years." She stopped at the surprise on Matt's face, wondering what was going on.

3

Jake couldn't believe he'd run into Heather, here of all places, in the motorcycle museum in Sturgis, South Dakota. The last time he'd seen her was just before his family had moved out of Mobile, as they'd followed his dad on the first of what had turned out to be many moves. Thankfully, he'd only had a couple of years left at home before he'd joined the military and had moved out.

He'd moved just as much as his parents had after that, but at least it had been following his own life, and not theirs. He'd always regretted leaving Mobile though. In high school he'd always had a crush on the sweet redhead now standing in front of him, but hadn't had the nerve to do anything about it. Maybe that could be different now.

Jake turned to meet her cousin and couldn't believe what he was seeing. "You're one of the Kings?" He held out one hand. "Good to meet you, I'm Jake." He shook the newcomer's hand.

"I'm Iceman."

"I've heard of you. I didn't know you were from Alabama." Jake motioned toward Heather.

"I'm not. She is. But I didn't know anyone in the Souls was from there either."

"I haven't been back in a long time." He turned back to Heather, feeling guilty about ignoring her to talk to her cousin. "I'd hoped you were doing okay." Crap. He hadn't meant to say that. Now she knew he'd thought about her after they'd moved. And he had. A lot. But he hadn't planned on telling her that.

"I was for a long time, but I just needed to get away for a while. It seemed like a perfect chance to come up and visit my favorite cousin." She leaned over and rested her head on Iceman's shoulder, batting her eyes at him. Iceman rolled his eyes, but wrapped an arm around her shoulders and tugged her close.

"I'm glad you did. I missed you too."

Jake got the feeling he wanted to say more, but didn't because of how public they were, and maybe what he wanted to say was private. He wondered if Iceman would have said it if he wasn't here or if they were just around the Kings.

"We were just headed back to the park," Iceman said. "I guess we'll see you there?"

"I just got here, want to take a turn around the place then I'll be back. I need to be there before they start serving to make sure my men are lined out on how things work."

Iceman frowned for a split second then turned to Heather. "You ready?"

"Whenever you are, but don't rush on my account."

"I didn't. I'm done."

"Okay." She turned to Jake. "I guess we'll see you at the park then." She headed for the door.

Jake couldn't help but watch her go, hoping she'd be around long enough he could see if what he'd felt for her all those years ago was still there, and that maybe she felt something similar. He was determined not to let this opportunity slip past him. He wouldn't lose what might be his last chance at the only girl he'd wanted to spend time with before he'd been forced to leave her behind, not again, not if he could help it. He took hope that she was at the event with her cousin. Hopefully, it meant she wasn't with one of the Kings. And maybe open to something with him.

Jake wandered through the museum, reading plaques, and admiring some of the more extravagant bikes. He didn't know why, but he found his thoughts kept drifting back to Heather. It wasn't like he'd never thought of her. Several times over the years, he'd wondered what had happened to her, and hoped she was happy. Now it appeared his hopes had been for naught.

She'd had a hollow, almost haunted look in her eyes that made him want to pull her close, to tell her everything would be all right and then to shelter her from the world. That wasn't practical, and he knew that, but damned if he didn't want to.

He glanced at his watch as he walked through the last room of the museum, taking in the different bikes and looks as he noted he still had almost an hour until Miles told him he needed to be back. Did he want to do something else or maybe go back to the park and mix with the Kings? Hadn't that been where Iceman said they were headed? If he went back, he might get a chance to talk to her again, maybe ask a few questions. Find out if maybe he could see her again.

Granted five hours between Gillette and Dickenson might make it more difficult, but since when had difficult kept him from doing anything he actually wanted to do? Not since he'd been in high school wishing he had the nerve to ask out a certain redhead.

Now, he took his time as he made his way through the rest of the museum, even browsing through the giftshop, and dropping an extra fifty in the donation box before he headed back out to his bike. Time to put his regrets in the past and see if maybe Heather could be talked into seeing him again.

He considered options and tactics as he made the short ride back to the park, then walked his bike backwards into line with the rest of his brothers' bikes. Jake still hadn't settled on a plan when he spotted her, a can of beer in hand as she chatted with a couple standing with Lurch, Tuck, London, and Kerry. He couldn't help but smile, as he noticed that she fit right in, as if she hung out with club leadership all the time.

4

Matt waited until they were back to the park to start questioning her. "Are you sure he doesn't have ties to the club in Mobile? The one your dickhead ex got mixed up with?" he asked as he dismounted from the bike.

"While I can't be a hundred percent sure, I'd say ninety-nine percent sure." She handed him her helmet so he could secure it. "He was a nice kid. His folks moved him out of Mobile while we were still in high school, and he said today he hadn't been back. Aaron could have lied, but why?"

"Why? Because he is mixed up with those assholes and doesn't want you to know."

Heather fought the urge to roll her eyes. Usually, it was her being paranoid about anyone she didn't know being tied to that club in Mobile, but then again, she felt like she knew Aaron.

But did she? It had been so long since she'd seen him last. And while she thought she'd known him then, she also thought she'd known Mitch, and look how that had turned out. Her mind began to spiral. Was she wrong about Aaron? Was he here looking for her? Did he plan to take her back to Alabama and the hell she had no doubt waiting for her there?

She shook herself and told herself that was stupid. Aaron had always been the first one to step up and stand up for anyone being mistreated or bullied. While she had no doubt he'd changed in the interim years, she didn't think he'd changed that basic part of himself.

At least she hoped not.

She didn't want to think about what he would have had to go through to change what she considered such a basic, core part of him.

"I'm sure. He's not mixed up with them." She didn't tell Matt about her doubts, one person thinking them was enough.

Matt didn't respond but watched her a moment, as if trying to figure out what she was thinking. After a moment, he nodded.

"Let's go see what everyone's up to and find something to drink." He turned, waiting for her to join him before they headed into the park.

Heather took a deep breath and wrapped an arm around his waist, giving him a quick sideways hug before releasing her cousin to walk beside him. She appreciated the way he'd taken her in, and that he was doing everything he could to keep her safe. She straightened her shoulders and decided to push away thoughts of Mitch and his idiot friends in Mobile. Today was a day to have fun, and she was determined to do just that.

Their first stop was at the row of several coolers they'd brought down from Dickenson with them. She knew several of them held food, but just as many had drinks of all kinds.

"What do you want?" Matt asked.

"Did we bring any Northern Route?" she asked about her favorite craft brew, made by a brewery in Dickenson. She'd fallen in love with it the first time she'd tried it, now it was her beer of choice.

"Miles knows how much you and a couple of other women like it, so I'm sure it's here somewhere," Matt said as he opened one cooler, pulled out a coke and dropped the lid, pressing it closed with his knee before moving a couple of coolers down and opening that one. From the way he'd gone straight to the cooler with the cokes in it, she knew there had to be some kind of system for what was where, but had no clue what it was.

"What are you looking for?" Miles asked as he stepped up, a wide grin on his face.

"She wants that Phat Fish beer some of the girls drink," Matt said, digging through one of the coolers with one hand.

"The Phat Fish is in that one over there." Miles indicated the cooler at the end of the row.

"Thanks," Matt closed the one he'd been digging through and went to the one he'd indicated. After a moment of digging, he pulled out a can, closed the cooler and brought it to her. "Here. Want to find a place to sit, or you want to wander around a bit?"

"I'll mingle, you go have some fun. You don't need to babysit me all the time."

Matt didn't say anything for a moment, but watched her, one brow lifted, as if he was asking if she was sure. She used the hem of her shirt to wipe off the top of her can, then opened it and took a long pull before using her free hand to shoo him away.

"Now that you've run him off, what's your plan?" Miles asked after Matt had reluctantly wandered off.

"I didn't lie to him. I'm going to mingle." She scanned the park, wondering where to start, then spotted Ava and Cowboy to one side, talking with a couple she didn't recognize. Might as well start there. Maybe she'd learn more about Aaron and these Demented Souls they were getting together with.

She didn't understand the whole thing, the meeting up with another club, but she was only on the edge of the Kings, so it didn't matter if she understood how it worked. Besides, she didn't know how long she would be around anyway. But maybe she could get an idea of what kind of man Aaron was now, maybe learn a little bit about his friends.

5

Jake wandered from group to group, checking in with his brothers and their women, making sure they had everything they needed and fetching a few things when they didn't.

"Have you eaten anything?" London asked with one lifted brow when he stopped to check on Tuck and the others where they sat with Cowboy and Ava, the King's president's wife.

"Not yet. I'm headed that way now. I just wanted to make sure you all didn't need anything first."

"If we did, we can figure out where to get it. Get your food before it's all gone."

"No chance of that," Cowboy said. "The option you want might run low or out, but we never run out of food."

London tilted her head and turned her attention to Cowboy. "What do you do with the leftovers?"

"We find a local shelter wherever we are and donate them. If there isn't one or they don't accept donations of prepared food, then we pack it back up and take it back to Dickenson. We've got a place there that focuses on vets that we have a good relationship with. We donate to them often."

She nodded and turned to Tuck, both brows lifted. "I like that."

"I do too. We can get Lurch looking for a place like that we can work with in Gillette, and we'll see what we can find in Tucson, once we're down there."

"I'll take care of that here, at least the looking and finding out who to put Lurch in touch with," Jake volunteered.

Tuck nodded, but didn't say anything more. London looked at him, then toward the edge of the park where the large grill trailer sat, with several other tables nearby where the food was being served, then back to Jake, an expectant look on her face. He knew better than to argue.

"I'm going to go get something to eat. If you need anything, call out. I'll be around."

"It's not your responsibility to play host, Jake," she said, her voice gentle.

"Begging your pardon, ma'am. but since I'm the one who got this all set up and going, it kind of is."

"Leave him be, sweetness," Tuck said. "He's a big boy, he can take care of himself." He reached over and patted her hand, letting her know he was aware of her and what she was doing. A soft smile curved her lips as she turned and looked at him.

Jake wondered if someday he'd have someone look at him like that. He'd love it if it was Heather, but he knew better than to hold his breath. First, he had to get up the nerve to talk to her again.

He glanced around and found the rows of coolers and recognized some of them as the ones they had at the ranch. He headed for the coolers, grabbing an amber from a brewery in Wyoming. He'd tried several since moving to the ranch, and found he liked Black Tooth brewery the best. They were currently competing with Barrio in Tucson for his favorite.

After popping the top, he took a swig and looked around for Miles. He didn't have to look far, Miles stood less than a dozen feet away from the far end of the huge grill trailer the Kings had brought with them, overseeing things as two men cooked and two more worked on laying food out for the buffet line that from the looks of it would go down both sides of the table.

Jake made a wide arc, being careful to go around the grill so he didn't get in the way as he went to Miles.

"Need anything done?" Jake asked, as he stepped up beside the Kings' road captain.

"Nope, we've got it handled." Miles turned and looked at Jake, then back to where the men worked around him. "The only thing you can do is let people know we'll be serving at noon and the women go first, like always." Miles tipped back the coke in his hand, taking several swallows, before lowering the can and looking at Jake. "The Kings know the drill, and from what you said earlier, it's similar to how you guys do it."

"It is." Jake checked his watch again. He wanted to go straight to Heather, but knew if he did, he wouldn't finish making the rounds of everyone there. So instead, he turned and went in the direction opposite of where she stood near the presidents and started there.

By the time he made it through all the clusters of people, both Kings and Souls, there was still about twenty minutes until they began serving. He used the time to move closer to Heather. She no longer stood near the same people. That had made him wonder if she'd gone to him because she wanted to report something or if she just knew him and was being social.

Maybe his time in the military, then with the Souls had made him paranoid. But then again, he reminded himself that it wasn't paranoid if they were really out to get you and too often in the recent past, people had really been out to get him and his brothers.

Now he just considered his musings as looking out for himself and his brothers. And someone had to. Gizmo and Krissi had the club's tech needs under control in Tucson, but it had fallen to Jake to handle them here, and he didn't feel nearly as qualified as he should be.

More often than he felt he should need to, he found himself calling south for advice or help, but he'd rather call them and be sure the club was taken care of than try to skate by on his own and screw something up. Still, it left him feeling incompetent, more often than not.

"Fancy meeting you here," the voice of the woman he'd been thinking of drew Jake out of his thoughts. He turned to find her watching him.

"Hey, I was wondering where you'd gotten to." He gave her his best grin, as if he hoped to charm her out of her panties, and he did, but not like he did most girls. Most girls were a means to an end, for both of them. He wanted to get laid, and they wanted to fuck a biker. They both got something out of it, and neither had any illusions. But Heather wasn't like that.

Even if he hadn't known her so long ago, he would have known that. She didn't dress like any of the women who hung around a club, not the ones who belonged to one of the brothers or any of the many girls who hung around hoping for a ride on a bike, a biker or both.

Aside from that, there was something about the way she moved, the way she looked around, and seemed to always be on edge that screamed scared. Of what he couldn't be sure, not without asking, and it was too soon for that. Yes, they had a thread of connection, because they'd known each other so long ago, but that's all it was, a thread. Too thin and too fragile to risk breaking, at least not until he'd had a chance to try and strengthen it.

"Here and there. I've been around, mingling, as Matt calls it." She glanced around, then looked down at her watch. "We've got a little time till they eat, how about we wander around a bit and catch up?" She waved around the park.

"Sure, but are you sure you don't want to sit and talk instead?" He tilted the top of his head toward an empty picnic table not far away.

Heather shook her head. "I've had enough time sitting for a bit, and it will be another three hour ride home. I'd rather move around."

"You got it." He motioned for her to lead the way.

She hesitated, as if not wanting to be out in front, but a soon as she took off, he stepped up beside her. He'd only wanted her to decide what direction they'd be going. They walked several paces before either said anything.

"You guys moved to California, didn't you?" She didn't look at him as she spoke, but stared off into the distance.

"We did."

"What's it like there?"

There was something in her voice that told him it wasn't just curiosity. Something told him she'd longed to go there, to see it herself. And something, or someone had prevented it.

"Totally different than Mobile. As in an entirely different culture. I could say that it seemed like a different country, and it wouldn't be that far off."

"But at least you didn't have to learn a new language."

Jake couldn't help but laugh.

"I wouldn't say that was entirely true."

Heather looked at him and frowned. He could tell she wasn't sure if he was messing with her or not.

"While yes, they do speak English, it's an entirely different English than you speak in Alabama. And I'm not just talking southernisms. They have a whole different way of using the same language and I admit, it took me a while to catch on."

He shook his head and turned to scan the area, making sure nothing was out of place. And nothing appeared to be, but he did notice Iceman watching them. Jake wasn't sure if he was just keeping an eye on his cousin or if he was making sure Jake didn't do anything that might hurt her. Not that he would, but Iceman had no way of knowing that. At least not yet.

He planned to make sure they both knew he wouldn't do anything to hurt her, but they needed time to be sure of that, both of them would.

"What did you do after school?" he asked. "Did you go to college like you planned?"

The ghost of a smile curved her lips as he reminded her of the plans she'd made back when they were both little more than kids. "Yeah, I went to USA, got my degree, went to work." She shook her head as if she couldn't believe she'd done all that or maybe that she'd done all that and still landed here.

"What do you do?"

Her smile disappeared. "What I do now is nothing. I'm begging a bed off my cousin and hiding from a mistake." She turned to stare off in the distance.

"A mistake?" He couldn't help but ask, watching her in hopes she might tell him more.

6

"A MISTAKE," HEATHER REPEATED, still not looking at him. "But what about you? What brought you up here? You always swore you'd never go where it snowed." She hoped he'd let her move the subject of their talk to him. She didn't want to elaborate on her mistake.

She might eventually have to tell him, depending on how things went, but not now, and not here, where anyone might overhear what she felt was one of the biggest mistakes of her life. She hadn't lied to him about that. Mitch had been a mistake. Now she wished she could forget him, but that was impossible, at least until she was sure that neither he, nor any of his buddies, and she used that term loosely, were looking for her. Until she was certain she didn't have that chasing her, she had to be careful what she did and who she trusted, though Heather was ninety eight percent sure that Aaron had nothing to do with that group, what if she was wrong?

"After a few years of incredible heat, the snow looked a lot better. Then my president had to come and spend a year up here, so I came to support him. I got up here last fall, and found I really liked it, despite the cold and the snow. They weren't as bad as I'd anticipated." He lifted one shoulder and let it drop.

"Lurch had to spend a year up here?" she asked, she'd me the man, and his woman, earlier.

"No, it was Tuck. Tuck's the president of the Tucson chapter, our original chapter. Tucson is where I've been for the last few years. He had to come north and once he was here, they decided to start a new chapter. Lurch is the president of this chapter, the Gillette Chapter."

"And since Tuck is your president, you're going back to Tucson when he does. When is that?" She couldn't help the pang of disappointment that shot through her as she discovered that he wouldn't be around much longer. Somewhere deep inside she'd been hoping now that she knew he was in the area, she might get to see him again, reconnect, and hopefully this time in a deeper manner than they'd ever connected in the past.

"Tuck's going back next week, it's why we've got so many men here, it's some from Tucson and all of Gillette's chapter. They came up to have a little fun, then escort him home."

He didn't answer what she thought was the most important part. How long did she have until he left too?

"And you'll leave with him, or are you going back separate?"

He turned and gave her what, on anyone else, she would have called a flirtatious smile. But he couldn't be flirting with her, could he?

"I'm not going back, at least not to stay. I'm sure I'll go back for a while, maybe over the winter when there's not so much to be done here. I have some business down there I'll need to take care of, but it can wait."

Heather's head whipped around to stare at him for several seconds. She could only stand there, watching him as her mount refused to follow directions and say the words she was thinking. Finally, after what seemed like an eon, she managed to get the words out.

"You're not leaving?"

He watched her, the corner of his eyes crinkling slightly as a slow smile spread across his face. "Not planning to. I've decided I like it up here. Plus, I recently found this girl I'd like to see more of." He paused.

Heather held her breath while she waited for him to say it. Was he thinking the same thing as she had been?

"So, do you want to see me again? Can I talk you into letting me come up to Dickenson and taking you out some time?"

Heather's heart seemed to flutter in her chest and for a moment the world began to spin, then she remembered to breathe.

"Shit, are you all right?" Aaron asked.

She nodded, then spoke. "I'm okay, just not the brightest sometimes." She gave him what she hoped was a reassuring smile. "I'd love to go out with you." She wondered, not for the first time, what any man saw in someone as scattered and ditzy as she was.

"I'm glad to hear that, but now I'm worried about you." He looked around then led her to a nearby bench. "Here sit down for a minute. Are you really sure you're okay?"

"I'm sure. I'm just an idiot." She stared down at her hands as her face heated.

A finger under her chin gently lifted her face until she looked him in the eye.

"Hey, don't talk about yourself like that."

"But it's true."

"It may have been a long time since I've seen you last, but I know better than that. You're smart. You're witty and at times, you're funny as hell. We all have moments of doing stupid things, but I can't say I've seen you do anything like that, not since I found you again." His voice was soft, gentle in a way she wasn't sure she'd heard from a man, or at least one she wasn't related to, in far too long. "So tell me what happened."

Heather let her eyes drop, it was hard looking someone in the eye while you admitted to something like this. You never knew how they would react. Would he laugh? Would he think she was dumb? Worse, would he be pissed for some reason. She was too close to get away before he had a chance to hit her if it pissed him off. She moistened her lips then let it out. "I forgot to breathe."

He didn't move or say anything for long enough, she looked up at his face to gauge his reaction. There was a light in his eye that hadn't been there before.

"Are you telling me I take your breath away?"

Heather couldn't help but giggle at the thought. She hadn't thought if it that way.

"Well, that's not how I would have put it, but you're not wrong."

"There. That's better." His voice was still gentle, but he seemed... satisfied somehow.

"What's better?"

"Seeing laughter in your eyes. I like it a lot more than the anxiety or the fear. Fear's the worst. I hate seeing any woman afraid, but seeing it on your face is worse. It rips me apart." His eyes were gentle as his hand slid to one side to cup her jaw. "It makes me want to find whoever hurt you and teach them a lesson. They need to know how to treat a woman, but at the same time, whatever they did sent you here. Back into my life and I can't be too mad about that." One corner of his mouth lifted in a wry smile. "Talk about twisted logic, huh?" He watched her for a moment longer, then spoke again. "Better now?"

She frowned. "When did you see me afraid?" She didn't think she'd felt the usual fear since she'd run into him again, at least not that she could recall.

"When I spoke your name in the museum. Terror flashed across your face. It wasn't there for long, and gone as soon as you realized who I was, but I didn't miss it."

Heather stared at him for a moment as she thought back to the encounter less than two hours before. She remembered the way her entire body had flashed cold, then hot before she'd looked up and seen him. Had she let it show on her face? Why wouldn't she have? Up until the last few weeks, she'd never had a reason to keep what she was feeling off her face. Even now she wondered what was on her face and what he saw.

"I'm glad it was you." She forced herself to smile as she met his gaze. She hoped how happy she was to see him, and that he was interested enough to ask her out showed on her face. She didn't know if she could come out and say it, but he should know. She just didn't know how to make sure he did.

7

Jake watched the string of emotions play out across Heather's face. He couldn't help but wonder what she was thinking, but from the smile she finally settled on, he decided not knowing was okay, at least for now.

"I'm glad it was me too." He found himself smiling down at her. He fought the urge to pick her up, sling her over his shoulder and haul her to his bike and away from here. He wasn't particular about where they would go as long as it could be just the two of them. He wanted to talk to her without having to worry about what someone else saw, what someone else thought, or having her worry about either of those.

But he wouldn't. She was having some kind of trouble, he wasn't sure what yet, but he knew Iceman was watching out for her and he wouldn't leave her without that safety net, at least not until he was sure she had something in place to replace it.

He ignored the voice in the back of his head screaming that he wanted to be that thing in place to replace the safety net that was her cousin. He hadn't seen her in too long. He wasn't in a position to take on what could be a big responsibility, depending on what she was so afraid of.

"How do you like it up here?" he asked, looking to keep the conversation light. He wanted to see her smile again. He liked that far more than the haunted look she wore now.

"So far, I like it. The weather is mild, not the sweltering steamy heat I left behind." Her cheeks turned pink, and he wasn't sure if it was because she was happy or because she'd thought of whatever had driven her out of Alabama.

"That's one thing I never missed about Mobile."

"The heat?"

"No, the humidity." He reached down and wrapped one hand around hers, then tugged her up and along as he continued walking along the perimeter of the park. He was afraid if they stood still too long then they'd draw someone's attention, and he got the feeling Iceman didn't like him talking to Heather.

Jake didn't know if it was because he was a Demented Soul or if Iceman was just that protective of her. And just like that he was once more wondering what kind of trouble she'd managed to find.

"It gets hot in Arizona, and I got used to that heat but it's different, and I know this is said all the time, but it's a dry heat. It's hot yes, but without the humidity, it's different. Not that it doesn't get warm here, but again, it's different. Here it doesn't stay hot long, you might get a few days of it then it cools off again. Not the months of heat and humidity you get on the gulf coast or the months of steady scorching heat in Arizona. I've found I really like the variety."

"I guess I understand that," she said after a moment. "It's still a novelty me, and I don't know what I'm going to do, long term. Only that I'll have to figure something out. I can't stay on Matt's couch forever."

He was about to ask if she wanted to talk about it when someone called his name across the park. He looked up and saw Iceman headed their way.

"Speaking of, isn't that him?" Jake tilted his head toward the man coming toward them at a jog.

"Yeah. Wonder what's up and while I'm wondering, why do they call you Jake? That's not even your middle name."

He turned and smiled at her, wondering when she'd ever heard his middle name. It had probably come up in some discussion in their group of friends in school, but he didn't remember when, but now that he thought about it a moment, he knew hers was Linnette. Why it popped into his head now, he couldn't say or when he'd learned it. But he did recall calling her a shortened version of her middle name back then. She'd probably learned his middle name at the same time he'd learned hers. Before he had a chance to ask, Iceman came up beside them.

"There you two are." He looked back and forth between Jake and Heather, as if trying to figure out what they'd been talking about then, after a moment he turned to Jake. "Lurch is looking for you."

Jake scanned the park, looking for the man he had to remind himself was president now.

"Did he say what for?" Jake asked, not spotting him right away.

"No, just that he needed to talk to you." Iceman pointed to one side. "He was over there a few minutes ago."

"I better go see what he needs." Jake turned and looked at Heather. "Can I look for you after I figure out what's going on? We can talk a little more about those plans we were talking about?"

Her cheeks turned pink, and she met his gaze for a moment before looking down at where their hands were still clasped.

"I'd like that."

"Me too. I'll find you before we head out today." He lifted their joined hands and kissed the back of hers before releasing it and going in search of Lurch. He didn't spare her cousin a second look as he headed in the direction Iceman had indicated.

"What do you mean plans?" Iceman asked as Jake walked away.

He didn't hear her respond, though for a moment, he wished he hadn't been moving so fast and caught what she'd said. But no, he'd been in a hurry to get this done so he could get back to her. Either way, she wanted him to find her again. He would take care of whatever Lurch needed then do just that.

8

Heather watched Aaron walk away, wondering what he was thinking and if he was really as interested in her as he seemed. She'd thought he was just being friendly but the way he'd kept his gaze locked on hers as he'd kissed the back of her hand made her think maybe she'd been wrong.

"What plans, Heather?" Matt's voice was impatient as if he'd asked the question before and he was tired of her not answering him.

"I'm sorry, I was thinking. What was that?" She turned her attention to her cousin, frowning at the scowl he wore as he watched her.

"What plans?" His voice was more than a little impatient.

"Aaron asked me to dinner."

Matt let out a mirthless laugh. "Our clubs split the cost of this meal, and the prospects have cooked it, under Miles supervision. Inviting you to eat it is not all that impressive."

"Oh. Not this one. Dinner some other day. We haven't decided when or where yet. That's what he meant about talking more about it." She turned and looked in the direction Aaron had gone. "We'll figure out the details then." She turned and looked at him again, wondering why he looked so unhappy. "What's wrong?"

"Are you sure this guy isn't mixed up with your ex or any of the men he's mixed up with?" He watched her a moment as if waiting for some reaction.

She tilted her head and watched him for a moment, "Didn't we just do this." She circled one finger in the air. "Only the other way around? Weren't you the one assuring me that the Demented Souls are allies to you and your friends so they're safe?"

"Yeah." Matt's scowl grew deeper. "You seemed to have a lot more self-preservation then. I'm not sure what changed that."

"I don't know." She rolled her eyes as she fought the urge to shove him. If she didn't know better, she would think he was jealous, but he was her cousin, so that was out. "Maybe that I knew him? Maybe I trust your judgement. I don't know why you seem to suddenly not be so sure they can't be trusted when you were the one assuring me, they are."

"I'm not worried about the whole club, just him." Matt glanced in the direction Aaron had gone, eyes narrowed, as if he was suspicious. "I don't like that it just happened that you knew one of them."

"It is odd. But it's not like he's been around Mobile for years. He and his family left before we graduated high school. And it's not like he showed up in this part of the country since I came up here."

"What do you mean?" Matt's head whipped around to watch her.

"He's been here since sometime last year. Said he'd come up before the winter really hit, and as much as he always thought he would hate the cold, he didn't mind it so much and it made a nice change from the heat. He's been in Arizona for a while before this. At least that is what he said. Something about coming up to support his president when he had to spend a year up here. But that year's up now. At least that's how I understood it."

Matt narrowed his eyes and turned back in the direction Aaron had gone. "They've got some men up from their other chapter, only been here a week or so and will be going home soon. I had assumed he was one of them. Which made his being here just after you got here more suspicious. If he's been here that long, then maybe it's not the issue I feared. Still. I'm going to keep an eye on him. The whole coincidence of it makes me suspicious."

Heather watched him for a moment, wondering if he'd always been this protective and she'd somehow missed it or if it was something new. Was it something he'd started since she'd come to him looking for help and somewhere to hide for a little while? She wasn't sure, but she knew it would do her no good to question him, not about that, and not right now.

"Come on, let's go see if the food's ready. I'm hungry." She bumped her shoulder against his arm as she turned to head back toward where the rest of the two clubs gathered around a large gazebo with several picnic tables.

"Don't run into me like that," he said with a grin as he used both hands and one shoulder to playfully shove her way, as he'd been doing in response to her move for years.

"Well, if you weren't so big you were in the way all the time, I might not run into you so often." She couldn't help the laugh that bubbled out, and she didn't try. She loved the playful side of their relationship. That, and knowing he would help her if he could, was what had sent her up here when she'd needed help.

Thinking of how he'd been there when she needed help sent her mind back to the moment she'd known she had to get out of Mobile. She'd been in the grocery store when she'd overheard voices that had sounded vaguely familiar. They'd reminded her of someone Mitch had brought over to the house a couple of times. Since she'd had her earbuds in, though they hadn't been on, and she'd been dancing to the song that had been on repeat in her brain while she'd shopped, she'd done her best to appear not to recognize them as she'd listened to what they were saying.

They'd been talking about her, one telling the other that Mitch was trying to talk the president into taking her as payment for some debt. At first, she'd been unable to believe it had been her, or her Mitch they'd been talking about, but when one of them had called him by his last name, Coleman, then asked how he'd ended up with someone like her, she'd known, though she'd ignored him when he'd called her a hot piece of ass. She couldn't react to that one phrase and not the rest.

Instead, she'd finished with what she was doing near them, then moved on. Stopping in a couple other aisles to grab things so it wouldn't appear she had heard them and now was running, then she'd gone to the register and paid for her purchases.

After loading the few items she'd gotten, thankfully she hadn't gotten to the perishable aisles yet, she'd climbed up into her truck and gone straight home. There she'd grabbed a few things she couldn't bear to leave behind if she never got to come back, then got back in her truck and hauled ass out of town.

She'd made it as far as Jackson, Tennessee that first day. By then she'd been so exhausted she'd stopped and rented a room for a night at the first place she'd seen. The next morning, thinking a little more clearly, she'd called Matt and told him what was going on. At his instruction, she'd gone to a bank and pulled everything she could in cash, filled her truck with gas and got everything she could think of she'd need for the drive on her credit cards before locking them in the glove box so she wouldn't forget and use them. Since she'd already put her room on them, if Mitch or his friends were looking for her, they could already follow her to Jackson, but she'd make it harder to follow her anywhere else.

Shaking her head, Heather forced her mind back the present. She needed to pay attention to the here and now. Worrying about what had already happened would do her no good. Now she needed to think about what was happening in the present, and what she would do in the future.

By the time she and Matt reached the gazebo, people were starting to line up.

"Go ahead and join them, get something to eat," Matt said, waving one hand toward the end of the line. "I'll grab a couple of spots at a table."

"No, you should go first, I'll get the table," Heather said.

"Not the way it works around here. Women eat first. Look." He motioned again at the line.

She took the time to actually look at who was lined up and noticed there were no men. With a frown, she turned to look at Matt. "What?"

Matt shook his head before she had a chance to say anything more. "That's just how we do it, women eat first, or if it's a family event, women and kids. Then the guys eat."

"But what if there's not enough for everyone?"

"Then we've made sure the ones we care about are taken care of and given ourselves a reason to work harder and make sure there's enough for everyone next time. Go get your plate."

Heather shot him a glare to let him know she didn't like him bossing her around, but turned and joined the line for food. She was hungry and even if she didn't like being told what to do, she wasn't going to starve herself to prove a point.

9

"You need something, sir?" Jake asked Lurch when he finally found him.

Lurch turned and stared at Jake for a moment, as if confused. "No. Is there a reason you're asking?"

"I was told you were looking for me."

Lurch frowned and shook his head. "I said your name in reference, but I wasn't looking for you. If I needed you, I would have called or texted."

"Good to know. I'll go check on how lunch is going then."

He turned away and slowly made his way toward the edge of the parking lot where the grill was set up. Along the way, Jake scowled and wondered if Iceman had simply misunderstood what had been going on or if he'd deliberately given him a false message. But why? Maybe to get him away from Heather? But from what she'd said, Iceman was her cousin. If that was true, then his motivation couldn't have been jealousy. Then why had he sent Jake on a wild goose chase just to get him away from her?

It was odd, but Jake would give him the benefit of the doubt at least until he got confirmation that the King was trying to keep him away from her. And if he was, why would he? Did it have anything to do with why she'd looked so scared? Was Iceman the reason he'd seen that look of terror on her face at the museum?

If he was, Jake wasn't sure he'd let the alliance between the Kings and the Souls stop him from making the other man pay. He hated knowing she was scared and if he could do something about it, he would. And if it wasn't Iceman causing the fear, maybe the man would be willing to work with him to find who was, and put an end to it.

Jake reached the table where the prospects had laid out the food and double checked that everything looked to be in place. A glance around gave him Miles' location, so he checked with the other man.

"What do you need me to do?" Jake asked as he stopped beside Miles.

"I think we're good, at least for now." Miles barely glanced at him as he kept an eye on the last-minute preparations, then turned to call out, "LINE UP!" He watched as several of the women stood and began to make their way in their direction. "I could use your help after we eat."

"No problem, what do you need?"

"If you could oversee making sure all the plates, cans, bottles, that kind of thing, make it to the trash, that would be great."

Jake frowned. "Doesn't everyone take care of their own?"

"Yeah, but once in a while something gets missed. If you could just cruise around the place a couple of times, making sure we got everything picked up, that would be great. I hate leaving a mess for someone else to clean up, especially after bringing in a group this size."

"No problem. Are you sure that's all you need?"

"Yeah. After everyone's through eating, I'll have these guys," he tilted his head toward the prospects who'd done the bulk of the work, "finish cleaning up, then we'll be done until we call it a day, load up and head home. You'll want to make sure to send them back for your coolers before you mount up."

"Not a problem. I don't think we would have forgotten them, but it's good to have the reminder and of course I'll take care of policing the area. You've done so much of the work today. Thanks for that. I owe you. I'll have to return the favor for our next get together." Jake made sure Miles had his number so they could stay in touch and plan additional events between the two clubs, then wandered off. He wanted to find Heather again, and hopefully work out the details on that date.

He spotted her a moment later, standing near the rear of the line to fix a plate. It only took him a moment to approach her.

"Where are you planning on sitting?" he asked, resisting the nearly overwhelming urge to wrap an arm around her waist, tug her close so he could taste her lips.

"Matt's got seats for us over there?" She motioned toward the far side of the gazebo. "Want to have lunch with us? I'm sure if you go check with him, he'll save an extra seat then you can come back and get your plate with me."

He smiled. "I'll go check with him, then once you're back, we'll get ours." Unable to resist this time he bent, but instead of kissing her, because he didn't want to scare her or see fear in her eyes, he touched his forehead to hers like he hadn't done to anyone since leaving Mobile all those years ago.

Strange how the old habit that their group had somehow gotten into, he didn't even remember why they'd started it, came back to him. As soon as he'd touched his forehead to hers, he straightened and went in search of Iceman.

With her in line, it gave him a chance to talk to the other man.

"Is your problem with me specifically or do you not like anyone around Heather?" Jake asked as he stepped into the seat across the table from where Iceman sat.

"I don't know what you're talking about." Iceman stared at him as if he hadn't just lied to him.

"Sure, play it that way." Jake stared at him for a moment, knowing their time was limited until Heather came back with her food. "Tell me this, are you trying to protect her, or have you got a thing for your cousin? Do you think she'll ever return you feelings?"

The look on Iceman's face told Jake what he needed to know. It wasn't that Iceman was harboring some weird desire for her.

"Tell me what's up and we can work together to keep her safe."

Iceman narrowed his eyes and watched Jake for a few moments then spoke. "Her ex is a piece of shit. I don't have a lot of details yet, but it looks like he's mixed up with a one percent club, I don't know which one, she didn't remember the name. She overheard a couple of idiots talking about how he was making a deal. They'd take her in exchange for wiping out his debt."

Jake didn't bother to keep the surprise off his face. Though he didn't know why. Little surprised him anymore.

"What else do you know?"

"Not a whole lot for certain. She heard them talking about her, but they didn't know she could hear them. She acted like she couldn't, got the hell out and left town."

"When was that?"

"She left Alabama almost two weeks ago. It took her a few days to get up here and she's been staying with me since."

"Do you know the name of the club?"

"No. she wasn't sure, and I haven't had time to look into it when she wasn't with me. She gets anxious when left alone for too long and sometimes it's all I can do to go to work. I've called in a couple of times because I couldn't leave her like that." He turned and watched the woman in question. Jake assumed it was not only to make sure she was okay, but to be sure she wasn't approaching and might hear them talking about her. "She didn't want to come today because she was afraid your club was tied to them, I convinced her it would be safe and that she would be surrounded by me and my brothers and would be safe. Then by chance, someone she knows from down there is here. How can I not draw conclusions?"

Things were becoming more clear to Jake. "Until I walked into that museum and saw her, I hadn't seen her or heard anyone speak her name since my family left Alabama roughly twelve years ago. I was just as surprised to see her as she was to see me. And the look of terror on her face before she spotted me just about gutted me." He took a deep breath and forced himself to continue. "I've thought about her over the years. I want to help her in any way I can." He wasn't going to admit to this near stranger how he felt, at least not all of it. But he needed her cousin to trust him. To tell him what he knew so Jake could help protect her. So he could make sure she was safe. He needed to do that, even if he could never have what he wanted from her.

And he wanted now, a hell of a lot more than he'd wanted twelve years ago. More than he'd known existed twelve years ago. But did she want it? That was what mattered.

No. What mattered first was making sure she was safe. He also wanted her happy but happy came second to making sure she was safe. Somewhere farther down the line was wanting to be with her, so far he wasn't considering it right now.

"Tell me what you know, before she gets here."

"I already did. That's all I know."

"You said she didn't know the club, do you know the ex's name?"

"Mitch Coleman. She'd been seeing him for the better part of a year, had moved in with him. She said she went home, knowing he wasn't there, grabbed a few things and got the hell out of Dodge. I didn't know until the next morning. She stopped for the night, slept then called me."

"Do they have anyway of tracking here up here?"

Iceman turned and watched Heather again. She was getting closer to the table where all the food was laid out, which meant they were running out of time.

"Maybe. I don't know what kind of resources they have. I've been hoping that it's been this long, they're not following her, but I can't count on that." He turned back to look at Jake. "I had her take some precautions, but there were others I just couldn't risk."

"Tell me." Jake pulled out his phone so he could make notes of anything he'd need to check.

"I had her pull cash and use that after she called me from Tennessee, but I couldn't have her get rid of her phone. I needed a way for her to call me or to call for help if she had trouble on the road. And her truck is only a few years old. I don't know if it has any kind of tracking in it. Fuck, it just occurred to me that the asshole could have planted some kind of tracker in it. I didn't even think to check it."

"But you said it's been almost two weeks, so one might think that if they were looking to get her back, then they would have made it up here by now."

"That's possible. It's also possible she's just a low priority at the moment or they're waiting for her to let her guard down. Maybe waiting for the heat to die down on something else or even this. The longer they wait, the less it seems like them when they do snatch her." Iceman shrugged. "I don't know these guys, and she said she'd only met them a couple of times, but they gave her the creeps. Said they talked about things no one who cared about staying out of jail would say in front of someone they weren't sure wouldn't turn them in."

Jake was quiet for a moment as he considered that. He and the Demented Souls were careful what was said around anyone, not about the things that could be criminal, but about the things that could get them killed. The criminal stuff that had to be proven, or at least they had to have evidence of some kind. Maybe knowing that had made this club, whatever it was, bold.

"Good to know. What else do you know? Is the club from Mobile or maybe one of the surrounding areas?" MC's and even motorcycles had barely been on his radar the last time he'd been in the area. Hell, he'd considered himself lucky to have the old beater pickup he'd worked his ass off for the summers of his freshman and sophomore years to buy.

They talked a little more, Jake taking down all Iceman could tell him. He'd do some inquiring once they got back to the ranch.

As Heather approached, they changed the subject, Jake asked Iceman how long he'd been in the area as she sat down, not next to him as he'd hoped, but beside her cousin. Maybe with time he'd get her more willing to come over to his side.

10

"Don't bother trying to fool me. I know you were talking about me and what's going on." She met Aaron's gaze as she spoke, then turned to Matt. "I thought we were going to keep this quiet."

"We are keeping it quiet, but if you're going to be seeing him, he needs to know. Besides, he was from the area, he may know some of these guys. He might be able to help," Matt said.

"I've not been in touch with anyone I knew from school, but I've got a couple of buddies from when I was in the Army who settled down there after they got out. I'll reach out to them, see what they can tell me," Aaron said.

She started to say something, she didn't know if it was say that wasn't necessary or to caution him about being too specific with what he was looking for. He held up one hand, letting her know he wasn't done.

"I'll be careful. I won't give your name or any details, but I can do a little fishing and see what I can find out. I'll do a little looking online too, see if I can figure out who these guys might be and if they're even looking for you." He gave her what she thought was a hopeful smile. "For all we know, they've written you off as gone for good and have moved on."

She watched him for a moment, trying to decide if he was lying to make her feel better or if he really believed what he was saying. After a moment she nodded, accepting it. She didn't think he was lying or at least not outright. He might be fudging the truth a bit, but she didn't know him well enough to be sure anymore.

"I thought we were told no poaching?" A blond with his hair pulled back onto a low ponytail and a couple months growth of beard came up behind Aaron and demanded.

Aaron turned his head far enough he could likely see the new guy, at least enough to identify him, if he knew him.

"No. *You* were told no poaching. But there are two differences here." Aaron kept his voice even, as if he was trying to teach the other man something.

"What? And don't tell me you're not trying to pick her up. I heard enough earlier to know you're making plans to take her out." The newcomer sounded defensive.

"Ok, let's make that three differences. We'll start with number one being that I know Heather, and not just from today. We knew each other years ago and just ran into each other again."

The new guy waved one hand as if dismissing that, but he didn't get a chance to say anything as Aaron continued.

"Number two being that Heather doesn't belong to any of the Kings."

"She's here with him." The new guy flung one hand in Matt's direction.

"Yes, she is, but she's not his ol' lady or even his date. She's his cousin."

Heather was glad he didn't go into detail about why she was here if she wasn't seeing one of the Kings. She didn't need her troubles spread wide for everyone to know.

The new guy, obviously one of Aaron's club members, folded his arm across his chest and scowled. She didn't have to know him to see he wasn't impressed by Aaron's reasons.

"And then there's the third, and maybe the most important one." Aaron stopped, glancing at her before turning back to look at the new guy.

"Enlighten me." The new guy's tone said he'd lost interest, but knew he wasn't getting away until Aaron had finished with whatever he was saying.

"The third difference is I asked Heather to dinner as a chance to reconnect, to get to know her and possibly build some kind of relationship. You don't do relationships with women. You hook up. And hooking up or trying to hook up with any woman associated with our allies is asking for trouble. That is why you were told no poaching."

"But you get to?"

Aaron shook his head. "No. I just explained to you why my asking Heather to let me see her again wasn't poaching. If you don't see the difference, it's because you don't want to. I'm not wasting more time trying to get the blind to see." Aaron turned back to face the table, effectively dismissing the stranger.

The stranger frowned at Aaron's back, opened his mouth like he was going to say something then shook his head, closed his mouth, and walked away.

"He's a player?" Matt asked once the stranger was gone.

"Yeah, Sackett will nail anything that walks. Once. Thankfully, it's not something I have to deal with much anymore."

"Oh?"

Heather stayed quiet as she watched the two of them talk. At least they were getting along now, and Matt wasn't doing his best to run Aaron off.

"He's only up for another few days. He'll go back to Arizona when the Tucson chapter leaves," Aaron said.

"And you're staying?" Matt's tone made it clear that he wasn't sure if he liked that.

"I moved to the ranch last fall. About the time of that dust-up with your previous president, if I recall right. I wasn't sure when I came up, but I have been for some time now. I've got no intention of leaving, at least not any time soon." Aaron met her gaze and winked as if he'd knew Matt was checking on his intentions toward her and possibly checking to see if he'd come up here looking for her for the men in Mobile.

"I told you." She tilted her head sideways until it knocked into Matt's shoulder. "Now, one or both of you go get a plate, before there's nothing left."

"Go ahead." Matt nodded at Aaron, letting the other man go first.

"You sure?"

"I'm sure." Matt made no move to get up.

"You know, I'm a big girl and with all these rough bikers around, I doubt anyone will brave the group to harass me. You can both go fill plates. I'll be okay." Heather was getting tired of their shit.

Matt looked at her as if he was trying to decide if she was telling the truth, then without a word he stood, looked at Aaron and tilted his head toward the line that no longer had any women, but was about a third of the men gathered around.

Heather looked around, noticing that even with food being served, there were men wearing the leather vests like Matt and Aaron both wore, scattered around the area where everyone gathered. They didn't look like they were standing guard, but she got the feeling they were making sure there was no trouble, from either inside the group or from anyone not part of either club. Feeling reassured, she picked up a tortilla from her plate, tore a chunk off and scooped up some of the beans before popping them in her mouth.

She blinked several times as she chewed and swallowed. The food was good, at least what she'd tasted so far, but she hadn't been expecting sweet beans.

"Is something wrong?" a woman's voice asked from not far away.

Heather picked up her coke, took a drink and turned to find a woman she'd seen a few times today, but didn't know her name.

"Yeah, I'm good. Thanks. I just wasn't expecting the beans to be sweet. It was a bit of a surprise."

The other woman frowned. "Why wouldn't they be sweet?"

"No reason for them not to be, I just wasn't expecting it. They're good I'm just not used to it, and didn't think about them being any different than what I'm used to. Thanks for checking on me though." She smiled and hoped the woman would take the hint.

Heather ducked her head and kept her gaze on her plate as she continued to eat. She'd been social and friendly all day and could use a few minutes of not talking to anyone to recharge, just a little. Not that she minded being around Matt, or even Aaron. She felt like she still knew him as well as she had way back when, even though they hadn't seen each other.

Was that odd? Did he maybe feel the same way? She couldn't tell, and she'd never ask, but she could hope.

11

By the end of the day, Jake didn't want to leave. Correction. He didn't want to leave Heather behind. He didn't want her to go three hours north while he headed a couple of hours west. He hated that there would be so much distance between them. Again.

But there was nothing he could do about it. It wasn't like he even had a place to bring her, should he take her back to the ranch. He lived in the bunkhouse with the rest of the single men. Even if he could convince her to come be with him, he had nowhere he could take her. Nowhere she would be comfortable at least. And he was not moving her into the bunkhouse with a half dozen crude, rough men who, half the time, had the manners of the wildlife they sometimes encountered when dealing with the ranch.

And as much as he wanted her closer, he didn't even ask. They'd only just reconnected and while he was far more confident than he'd been the last time he'd known her; it was too soon for that. No matter how badly he might want her closer. No matter how badly he might want to make sure she was safe. No matter how worried he might be.

No. He had no need to worry. Iceman and the Kings were watching out for her. He had no reason to believe they couldn't keep her safe. But he could help, by looking into what was going on in Alabama. That he could do.

At the gas station, fueling up before leaving town, Jake pulled up his contact list and sent a message to an old buddy. One he hadn't heard from in a while, but didn't doubt would be there when he needed something.

Jake: Hey how you doing?

He stared at the screen while he waited for his tank to fill but didn't have much hope. Maybe he'd have a response before he got back to the ranch.

Jake pocketed his phone, took one last long pull from the water bottle he'd snagged from the cooler as they'd loaded them up before leaving and tossed the empty bottle before putting the gas pump away and moving his bike so someone else could get to the pump. Ten minutes later, one by one the Souls pulled out of the station and hit the road. He was looking forward to the ride to get out of his head for a bit.

⁂

THEY'D BEEN BACK AT the ranch for nearly an hour before he had time to pull out his phone. He intended to call Heather and check on her. They should be getting close to Dickenson by now. But he found a response to the message he'd forgotten he'd sent. Hoping his old buddy would be available and maybe have some information for him, he opened the message.

Hex: Yo, man, how's it hanging? It's hotter than Hades here, but I don't guess it's any better in Tucson, huh?

Jake checked when the message had been sent. Less than ten minutes before. How had he not noticed his phone vibrating? He debated for a moment whether or not he should but then hit the button to dial the number instead of typing up another message. It only took a couple of moments before he heard a familiar voice come across the line.

"Yo, how are things in the desert?" Hex said in greeting.

"Hot I'm sure, but I'm not there. I left Arizona last fall."

"I didn't know. Where are you now?"

"Wyoming. You still in Mobile?"

"Yeah, not planning on leaving any time soon."

"Still part of the Warriors?" Jake asked. Shortly after settling in the area, Hex had joined a club called the Savage Warriors. While Jake didn't know anything about the Warriors, he knew Hex well enough to know the man wouldn't be involved in what seemed to be going on around Heather.

"Yeah, you know how it is. You still with the Souls? Or was a split with them what sent you north?"

"I'm still with the Souls." He debated how much to say. The second chapter was no secret, but the why, that was Tuck's personal business and Jake didn't want to advertise that. "We chartered a second chapter. I moved north with the new chapter."

"Nice. You always swore you'd never go where it snowed, I guess that's changed, huh?"

Jake couldn't help the chuckle that escaped. "Yeah, after years of the heat I was ready for a change. I've been up here since last fall, and I realize I don't mind it so much. Yeah, it gets cold, but you can always add another layer or a better layer. People start complaining if you remove too much when it's hot. It's not fun."

Hex laughed. "You just looking to catch up or you need something?"

"I wish I could say I was just looking to catch up."

"But?"

Jake shook his head and wondered how Hex always seemed to know when there was something he wasn't saying. Was he leaving some clue out there that the other man was reading? He needed to figure it out so he could cover it, whatever the tell was. He took a deep breath and spit it out. He'd already determined how much he'd be willing to tell Hex, and what he would be keeping to himself.

"I've had some inquiries, and I need to know what you might know or if you can find anything out."

There was no response for long enough that Jake wondered if the call had been disconnected. He pulled the phone away from his ear and checked the screen. No, the call was still connected. He put it back to his ear and waited.

This time he didn't have to wait long.

"Tell me."

"I need to know anything you can find out on a guy named Mitch Coleman. We've been contacted about collecting on a debt he owes, and something seems off."

"What do you mean?"

"Why contact a club fifteen hundred miles away? Is he up here or what? Does he have some assets up here we're supposed to acquire? I'm not sure about the whole thing and before I let my club get involved, I need more information." He paused, wondering if he should say more. "Have you heard anything?"

"The name's not familiar, so I've not heard anything, but I can do some checking. What kind of place has been in touch? Any clues where to start looking?"

"I don't have much. One of the prospects brought it to me. Some connection of his brought it to him, said there was some kind of reward for collecting on this one, but he couldn't tell me much. He said some club down your way was looking for him to collect the debt. I googled the name and came up with one in Mobile and thought you might could help me find more details."

"I'll look into it. I can't guarantee I'll find anything, but I'll look. How's life up where it's cool?"

They chatted a while longer, catching up in a way neither had had time for in far longer than Jake cared to admit, then rang off. When he'd finished that call, he checked the gear from today, making sure the prospects had taken care of things like he'd instructed, then walked out behind the barn where he knew he wouldn't be overheard and dialed the number he'd been aching to call since he'd programmed it into his phone hours before.

12

Heather jumped when her phone rang, vibrating against her leg while the rock song she'd set as her ring tone played at full volume.

"You okay?" Matt asked.

"Yeah, it just startled me." She pulled the device from her pocket and checked the screen. Her heart seemed to skip a beat before speeding to what seemed like its normal usual pace. She swiped her thumb across the screen.

"Hello?" She hadn't even thought about not answering it, which was what she would have done if it had been Mitch, or an unknown caller, but this was neither.

"Hey." The voice that rumbled across the line calmed her nerves like nothing else had in days. It had been the same this afternoon, once she'd realized who it was calling her name. Something about him made her feel safe, even safer than being here with Matt, and that was saying something. Because for a long time, going several years back, at least until this morning, she would have said being here with Matt was the safest she'd felt since she was a kid.

Thinking about that made her miss her parents. Or at least the parents she remembered from her childhood. They were still around, but not the same people they'd been then. And it wasn't just her perception of them now that she was an adult.

After she'd moved out to start college her parents had split. She'd been able to see for a while that they weren't happy and had expected they'd be happier apart and even now she had to admit they were. But she hadn't been ready for the other changes they'd made.

If it had just been the ways they were living, that wouldn't have bothered her, but her father had married a woman only a few years older than her, and while he'd called her occasionally, he didn't seem interested in seeing her much. She didn't know if he didn't want others to know he had a daughter as old as she was or not, but that was the feeling she got. It had caused them to grow apart in ways she didn't have a remedy for.

Then there was her mother. That change took longer but was no less jarring than what had happened with her father. Mom had nothing nice to say about her father, and while that wasn't a huge change, in the nearly ten years since her parents' divorce, she'd only become more angry and bitter. It had gotten to the point that Heather actively avoided talking to her mother because she didn't want to hear an angry rant about her father or whatever male had pissed her mother off this week.

All the changes didn't keep her from loving her parents, but they had meant that when the problem with Mitch and those bikers he'd been spending time with came up, she hadn't been comfortable going to either for help.

"Did I lose you?" Aaron's voice in her ear reminded her of what she was doing and pulled her mind from her thoughts of her parents.

"No, I'm here. Sorry. I just got lost in my head for a moment. I'm glad to hear from you. I take it you had no trouble getting home?"

"None. That's part of why I was calling. I wanted to make sure you made it back safe."

"We did. No problems, at least not that I'm aware of." She glanced up and found Matt watching her, a crease between his brows. 'Aaron' she mouthed to him, before standing and started walking around the room while she talked. "It was a nice ride. We stopped once for a few minutes, but I think we made good time. How about you guys?"

"We've been back a while, even had time to get everything unloaded and put away. I waited to call to make sure you guys had enough time to get home. You had a longer ride than we did."

"Wow, not only home, but all unloaded too? You guys are on top of it." She had no clue if the stuff they'd taken today was unloaded or not. Matt wasn't part of whoever did that.

"I wanted to get it done so it wasn't waiting on us tomorrow," Aaron said. "What are your plans for the rest of the evening? Going to have a good time?"

"I don't know." She looked around, wondering how much attention Matt was paying to what she was saying. "I'm not sure I want to do much. I'm kind of hurting."

"I bet. If you're not used to riding much or at all, then you spent six hours on a bike, even broken up like today, it's likely to make you sore. I recommend a hot bath. Run the water as hot as you can stand, add a little Epsom salt to the water if you can get your hands on some, then soak for at least twenty minutes. That will help ease some of that soreness. Hang on a sec." He paused, and she heard him speak again, but his voice was muffled, as if he'd put his thumb over the speaker. She wondered if someone had come to talk to him, but before she could figure out how to ask without being rude, he came back. "Sorry about that. Have you checked to make sure you're just sore and don't have any saddle sores?"

"Saddle sores?"

"What hurts? The skin or the muscles? Do you have rubby spots from riding or just sore from sitting in a position you're not used to?"

Heather frowned, thinking about it. she wiggled her hips while considering where it hurt. "No, not my skin, but deeper. It's definitely my muscles that are sore."

"Good. Then do the bath thing, with the salts if Iceman has any."

"What would you have said if I said I have rubby spots?"

"I'd have told you to leave the salt out. The last thing anyone wants is salt in an open wound. The hot water would sting, but making it salty would hurt more. If you were here, I might could do more, but the bath will help. And drink water. Water will help flush out the lactic acid."

Heather frowned. It sounded like was making that up, but the more she thought about it, when you got a massage, they told you to drink water to flush out toxins, so what could it hurt?

"I'll do that," she said. She kind of wished she had someone to curl up against, to rest, to just be reassuring. Of all the things she could have missed from being in a relationship, that was the one that came up the most.

She'd thought as she was leaving Mobile that she would miss sex on a regular basis, or at least semi-regular, because that's what it had become with Mitch, but she'd barely thought about that since she'd been here.

"What's going through your mind?" Aaron's voice drew her back to the present again.

What was wrong with her tonight?

She debated telling him for a moment then decided she had nothing to lose. She'd already walked away from nearly everything she'd thought was important. Besides, what was the worst he could do? Laugh and tell her she was naive? She'd already figured that much out when she'd realized the creeps in the grocery store were talking about her.

"I was thinking what I really want is someone to curl up against. Someone who will let me lay my head in their lap and not expect anything but being close. Someone I can be that real with."

"I'd do that for you if I were there." He sounded like he meant it. Like he really wished he were here so he could do what she wanted.

"Really? You wouldn't want more?" Heather wished she could take that back. It sounded needy and like she was fishing for complements and that wasn't what she'd meant.

"Really. It's probably stupid to tell you this now, but oddly, it's easier over the phone. Probably because I can't see your face and see how you're reacting if you don't feel the same. But all those years ago? Before we moved away? I was trying to work up the courage to ask you out. Then I found out I was leaving and as badly as I wanted to, I couldn't. Not just because we were leaving, but what if you said yes, then I had to leave you behind anyway?"

"But you can tell me now?"

"Now I've already asked you out. And you said yes. Now I've learned that if you don't ask, the answer is always no. But if you take a risk, if you do the thing, if you ask the question, you might get a yes. It might work. I'd rather have a maybe yes than a definite no."

Heather's breath caught in her throat as she tried to figure out what to say. How did one respond to something like that? Not that he was wrong, or that she didn't agree. Quite the opposite. He'd said it so well. She swallowed and tried again.

"I like that." She had a hard time making her voice come out as more than a whisper, but she'd managed. Barely.

"If I was close enough, I'd come over, strip you down and put you in the tub myself. Then when you were done, I'd dry you off, dress you in your most comfortable pajamas and let you curl up in my lap and relax until you fell asleep." The low rumble of his voice sent a shiver through her body, even over the phone.

"I wish you were close enough to do just that," she said, as she headed down the hall toward her bedroom Matt didn't need to hear where this was going. If he did, he would give her shit about it later. Besides, he didn't seem to like Aaron, though Heather wasn't sure why. She didn't want to give him any more reason to dislike her friend, even if she hadn't been in touch for a long time.

"About that dinner. I wish I could say I could be there tomorrow. I'd love to see you as soon as I can, even tonight wouldn't be too soon. But we've got visitors, and I can't get away for that long until they're gone."

"When will that be?" Heather couldn't stop the pang of disappointment that shot through her. She'd been hoping to see him again in the next few days.

"They won't be leaving for another week. So, I can't make it up there until at least then. I'm sorry. If you were close, I could manage something, or I'd ask you to come out here. We've got things going on that I can't get out of, but I would if I could."

She made it into her bedroom, closed the door then sat on the edge of the bed, wishing there was a solution. "What kind of things do you have going on?" she asked, trying to keep him talking. She didn't care about what, she just wanted to hear his voice.

"We've got a couple more rides and a community event we want to turn out for."

"You get involved in community events?" she asked, not sure why this surprised her.

"We do. We want a good relationship with the people of Gillette, so we find events that we can contribute to, and go participate."

"What's this one?"

"They're going to have a demolition derby in town. Some of the guys have picked up an old beater, and have spent their free time fixing it up, putting a change in it. We've entered it. It's not much but it will be fun."

"Who's driving?" She thought about the men she'd met and who was most likely to be that kind of dare devil. It wasn't until he didn't answer right away that she realized what he wasn't saying. "Aaron?"

"Yeah?" His voice had turned hesitant.

"Please tell me you're not driving."

The silence coming across the line spoke volumes. But he didn't just ignore her. He did respond, just not in the way she'd hoped.

"Sorry, Lynnie. I was the only one willing to get behind the wheel."

Heather felt like her brain shorted out as the nickname she hadn't heard in more than ten years registered. No one had called her that but him. And she never would have admitted it then, but she'd liked it. She had given up on ever hearing it again. Now, it made her eyes water, and her insides turn to goo.

When had she become so soft and sappy?

13

Jake listened, wondering if he'd just screwed things over with Heather. He didn't know which part was worse, confessing that he was going to be driving the car for the demo derby or calling her by the smart-ass nickname he'd dubbed her with back when they were freshman.

He didn't check to see if the call was still connected, he could hear her breathing on the other end of the line. He didn't check on her. He just waited.

It took her almost ninety seconds to speak, and even then, her voice was soft and breathy as if she didn't believe what she'd heard. "You remembered."

"I never forgot, Lynnie. You still got a thing for gummy worms and red hots?"

She laughed. "Of course, but—"

"No sour worms," he finished the last of that phrase along with her.

They laughed together. The sound made him wish he didn't need to be here for the next week. It made him wish his brothers would go back to Tucson, despite how impatient he'd been for them to get here.

"You know," she said after a moment. "I get that you are tied up there, but I don't have anything holding me here. I can come down there and spend some time with you."

Jake opened his mouth to say no but stopped before he got the words out. He did want to see her. And without waiting long enough so he had time to get away and get all the way up to Dickenson.

But where would she stay? He didn't think she'd be up to setting up a tent in the back field with the visiting club.

"I'd love to see you, Lynnie. But I live in a bunkhouse. I don't have anywhere for you to stay. I mean I could find you a tent if you want to set up in the pasture like our visitors from the original chapter, but somehow, I don't think that's your style."

"Yeah, not really." She took a deep breath and let it out in a rush. "How far is the ranch from town?"

"About a half hour. It's not too bad, but I don't want you coming down and spending money on a hotel, at least not for more than a single night at a time." He didn't tell her that if anyone was spending that money, it would be him. He didn't want her putting a charge on any of her cards, just in case that douchebag Mitch had people watching her accounts in an attempt to find her.

"I don't want to do that either. I don't want to spend too much money until I have some coming in again. I've got something else in mind."

"What?" He wondered what she was thinking.

"No. Let me see if I can get it to work out before I tell you what I'm thinking."

Jake took a deep breath and shook his head. He knew better than to push for an answer before she was ready to tell him. He wasn't sure if there had been anyone more stubborn in the entire school than Heather had been when she'd made up her mind about something.

"All right, but if I can help with something, you'll let me know, right?" he said, hoping she'd agree. Sometimes she got something so set in her mind she wouldn't take what was freely offered. He hoped she'd gotten past that but knew better than to count on it.

"If I think you might can help, I'll say something. I'll even let you know what it is before I jump in feet first. I'm not as impulsive as I used to be. I just want to make sure it's feasible before I share."

She sounded so reasonable he didn't try to convince her otherwise. Instead, he hoped that either Iceman would be able to steer her in the right direction or she'd call and check with him before just showing up with whatever her wild scheme was.

Not that he knew she was still up to wild schemes, but the Heather he'd known years ago had come up with some of the craziest, and he had to admit, fun, things they'd done, and gotten in trouble for. And he hadn't regretted a single thing they'd done, partly because it had been time spent with her. Oddly, he suspected he'd feel the same way now.

He'd have to wait and see what she came up with and how he felt about following her into trouble. Or doing his best to keep her out of it.

Over the next couple of days, they exchanged a few calls and a lot of text messages, and while they both wanted to be able to see each other, neither had found a way to make it possible.

He was sitting around the campfire in the middle of the common area where people had taken to gathering one evening when his phone buzzed. Having a good idea who it was, he pulled it out and found he was right.

Heather: Busy?

Jake: Not especially, need something?

He watched the screen with a frown as bubbles danced, stopped, then started again a moment before a new message popped up.

Heather: Can I call?
Jake: Sure.

"Give me a minute," he said to the brothers he'd been talking to as he stood and walked away.

"Where's he going?" Savage asked. He'd been busy with Donna most of the time since they'd arrived.

"Must be time for phone sex," Malice put in.

Jake flipped Malice off as he walked away, then ignored the rest as his phone rang.

"Hey, Lynnie, what's up?" he said in way of greeting.

"I think I have it figured out, but I need to run a couple of things by you first, and you may need to get approval from your boss, or maybe the guy who owns the place."

Jake was stunned for a couple of moments, as it took that long for her words to process. "Okay, lay it on me. What's the plan?" He headed for the horse barn, wondering how in depth this plan was and how long it would take her to explain. He knew from experience that once she got started with a plan it could take her a while to express it.

14

Heather held her breath while she waited for Aaron's response. She'd spent the last day and a half convincing Matt to let her borrow his trailer, not that he'd put up any argument about her having it. No, his problem was that he didn't want her to go to Wyoming. He didn't want her spending time with Aaron.

If she didn't love him as much as she did, it might have come to more than just the words she'd had with Matt over his attempt to tell her where she could go and who she could see. In the end, just as she'd known she would, Heather had won, and he'd agreed to let her borrow his trailer.

"I think that will actually work. I'll have to check with Lurch, and maybe Tuck to be sure. Is the trailer 30 amp or 50?"

She wasn't sure she liked how surprised he sounded when he said it might work. Did he expect her to come up with something that wouldn't work?

"Um, I'm not sure. Let me ask." Heather went to the bedroom door, opened it, and called out, "Matt!?"

"Yeah?" His voice came back from the front room.

"Is the trailer 30 amp or 50?"

"50."

"Thanks!" She closed the door and put the phone back to her ear. "Did you hear that?"

"No I only heard your side."

"He said it's 50."

"Good to know. I'm not sure we've got an outlet that will plug into, but I'll look into it. I also need to ask permission."

He seemed to be saying that last to himself, though Heather got it. You didn't just set up a trailer on your boss's land without at least asking first. Much less do it when some stranger would be staying there.

"How long you planning to stay? They're going to want to know."

"I don't know. I don't have anything keeping me here. I only came here to get away from Mobile and what was after me there. I can settle there as well as here. Maybe I can look around and find a job." She didn't know if he even wanted her around that long, but what if he did?

"I'd like that, but let's not start off telling Lurch that."

"Would he have a problem with it?"

Aaron snorted. "Not likely. You met him the other day, right?"

"I think so." Honestly, she'd met so many people that day she couldn't match names and faces in her head.

"He's the guy with the Cajun accent."

Coming from Mobile, she'd heard her share of Cajun, and with that descriptor, the man in question's face popped up in her mind's eye. "Oh yeah. I know who that is. I talked to him and his wife, but I don't remember her name either. There were just too many new people that day."

"No worries. Her name is Kerry, but that wasn't the point. Any way he met a girl and moved her onto the ranch. So did Tuck, but since it's his place, and they're getting ready to go back to Tucson, I 'm not sure that counts. Anyway, since Lurch and Kerry got together, we've had a couple of the guys who've found women that stuck. They've moved them into cabins on the ranch and it's not been a problem."

She wondered if there was a reason he didn't have a cabin. Were they only built once there was someone to move into them? She had so many questions, but wasn't going to ask them, not yet anyway.

"So how soon will you know?"

"A couple hours, tops, but I don't want you coming all this way tonight. Is Iceman bringing the trailer?"

"Hell no." She didn't tell him she'd had to argue with Matt about what she was going to do or that he didn't want her there. "I'll bring it."

"You good towing?"

She had to remind herself that he didn't know what she'd been up to for the last ten years. He had no way of knowing that while yes, she'd gone to school, she had since found that she liked working with her hands better than being in an office. Fortunately, she'd found the best of both worlds when she'd decided to become a vet tech. In the south, that meant horses and sometimes cattle. She'd driven more trucks towing horse trailers, with a variety of passengers, than she could count.

Thankfully, her boss, Brandon, had been understanding when she'd called and told him she needed some time off. She'd told him it was a family emergency, and that she had to leave town and didn't know how long she would be gone, or if she was even coming back. He'd told her to take as long as she needed and if it ended up that she wasn't coming back, he'd give a good recommendation wherever she landed. She seriously loved that man, but he was a good thirty years older than her, and head over heels for his husband.

Wyoming was ranch country. She wondered how hard it would be to find a vet looking for some help.

"I can tow, no problem." She might tell him more, later. If he ever asked.

Who was she fooling? He'd ask, it was just a matter of time. They'd been apart for so long; he simply hadn't had time to ask about every detail of her life. And it wasn't like she'd asked enough to know more than the vaguest idea of what he'd been up for all this time.

"Okay. I'll take your word for it. Either way, it's too late in the day to start that trip. I'll talk to Lurch and get the okay, and let you know. You can take off tomorrow, or even the next day if you need longer to pack up and get ready. I want to see you, but I want you safe and comfortable more."

Warmth pooled in her chest. She loved that he cared that she was safe, and that she felt safe. She couldn't remember Mitch every telling her to be safe or even asking if she was okay. No, he'd dragged her along to meetings with those friends of his who talked about her as if she couldn't hear them. She'd been more than uncomfortable, but when she'd asked to leave, Mitch had put her off. After that, she found reasons not to go along if she knew that was where he was headed.

"Will do. In the meantime I'll start getting things ready. I'll need directions for once I'm close. I can make it to Gillette, but I'll need to know how to find you once I'm that close."

"I'll send that once I've got clearance from the boss. You sure you're good with the trailer on your own? I can leave early and come help."

"And then we'd have two vehicles here to get back. No. I'm good with the trailer. It won't be my first rodeo."

"What kind is it? Bumper tow, fifth wheel?"

"Technically it's a fifth wheel."

"Technically?"

"Matt's modified it so now it's a goose neck, which is good because my truck's not set up for fifth wheel."

"But it is for gooseneck?"

"Yep." She decided not to elaborate. If he wanted to know, he would ask. But maybe he didn't want to know. Maybe he assumed it was like that when she'd bought it. He also hadn't seen her truck, so he had no reason to be curious about it.

"What have you been up to, other than trying to talk Iceman in to letting you come down here?"

Heather frowned. "How did you know?"

"Know what?"

"That Matt tried to talk me out of going."

"Lynnie, I talked to him at the run the other day. I know he's worried about you. I am too."

"I'm a grown woman. I can take care of myself."

"I know that, and so does he. It's not you taking care of yourself we're worried about. It's you trying to take care of that asshole you were seeing or some of the fuckers he was mixed up with, and failing. That's what we're worried about, and it's because we care."

The fight in her deflated like a balloon with a hole in it. How did you fight back against 'because we care'? What kind of comeback was there for that? She didn't have one and wasn't sure she wanted to come up with one.

"I know. It just rankles. It feels like you're both telling me I can't do anything without a babysitter, and I haven't needed a babysitter in longer than I want to think about."

"I'm sorry. That's not what it is, and I'm sorry it feels that way. We're just trying to make sure you're safe from that fuckwad. Are you carrying?"

Heather blinked. "Carrying?" What on earth did he want her to carry? She had a pocketbook, of course, but what else would he want her to have?

"Are you armed?"

"Oh. No. I hadn't even thought about it."

"Do you have one in your truck?"

"No." She frowned again. Her dad had kept a pistol in his truck, but she never had, she'd never seen the need.

"Do you remember how to shoot?"

"Of course."

"How long has it been since you've been shooting?"

"A few years, why?"

"I need to talk to Iceman."

Heather frowned. "Why?"

"I want to make sure you're protected. Is he around?"

"Yeah, let me go get him."

"Thanks, Lynnie."

Heather left the guest room she'd been sleeping in for the last couple of weeks and went in search of her cousin. She found him in the living room in front of the TV.

"Aaron wants to talk to you." She held out her phone. Matt scowled but took it.

"Yeah?"

15

Jake didn't like the idea of Heather on the highway on her own, unarmed. Especially if they didn't know anything about this Mitch or the men he'd apparently bartered her off to, or where they were.

"Hey," he said when Iceman got on the line. "You have plans for this afternoon?"

"Not really, why?"

"You got time to take Heather out for a little target shooting? And possibly have or can get your hands on an extra pistol to let her carry for a while? She's just let me know she's unarmed. I don't like it. Not with that asshat on her tail and especially not if she's going to drive down here on her own."

"I'm with you on this one. I'll make the time and yes, I've got something she can borrow. I'm not sure what yet, but we'll figure it out. She'll be protected."

"Good. I've got to talk to Lurch and get permission to park on the ranch. I'll be in touch about that as soon as I get the details. She's already agreed to wait until tomorrow to hit the road. Did you know she can tow? Will she be okay bringing your trailer down?"

Iceman chuckled. "Yeah. I knew. She'll be fine, or I would make sure she'd have help."

That made Jake feel better about her driving down here on her own. Iceman had known her the whole time he'd been out of the picture. If he trusted her with his trailer, who was Jake not to?

The other man continued. "I'm not sure if you've figured it out yet, but she does not take being told no well."

He heard the smack of skin against skin, as if someone had been smacked upside the head, then Heather's voice came over the line, but not like she had the phone. It sounded more like she was nearby, talking so they would both hear.

"Stop talking about me as if I'm not here."

"Geeze, stop hitting me, woman. Don't make me have to sit on you."

Jake clenched his teeth to keep from saying something he would regret as he reminded himself Iceman was her family. He wouldn't do anything to hurt her. He was trying to protect her and crap like what he'd just heard was nothing more than a squabble among cousins who'd grown up doing the same thing.

"I'll take care of it. You get her the details on whether or not she can park the trailer there and I'll make sure she's safe to go."

"Thanks, man. I owe you." Jake hated admitting he owed anyone but for Heather, he'd do it.

"No, you don't. Just make sure she stays safe, and you don't hurt her, and that's all I need."

"You got it."

"I'll let you talk to her again. I'll get your number from her and send you a message so we can stay in touch, in case that asshole shows up here."

"I appreciate it."

The line went quiet for a moment and Jake couldn't help but wonder what was happening in Dickenson. Had she muted the line to read Iceman the riot act? He hoped not but he knew if she had, he was likely in for the same treatment. Not that he blamed her, and he'd do it again, to make sure she was safe, but she'd rather have her here in front of him while she did it.

If he had to listen to her tell him how she was a grown woman who could take care of herself, then he would prefer he be able to see the fire in her eyes while she did it. And from the way she'd said the same things in high school, he had no doubt it would be coming, the question was when.

After a couple of minutes, Heather came back on the line.

"So I guess I have plans this afternoon," she said in greeting.

"I'm not sorry, Lynnie. I want to be sure you're safe. Knowing your armed and know how to use it will make me feel better about you driving down here alone."

"I will be fine. I drove myself all the way up here, didn't I?"

"You did, and I love that. I'm so glad to see you again. Besides, since when do you not enjoy an afternoon at the range?"

"Never, but that's not the point."

"Then what is?" He didn't want to fight with her. He wanted to know that if shit happened, she could handle it.

"That you went behind my back and arranged it."

"Sweetheart, if I'd gone behind your back, I wouldn't have asked you to give him the phone. I would have gotten his number and contacted him without you knowing."

"Then why did you have to talk to him instead having me do it?"

"Because I wanted the request to come from me. I wanted him to know I'm doing what I can to make sure you're safe." He pinched the bridge of his nose and made a silent plea for patience. He could do this, he wanted to, but he wasn't used to explaining himself, at least not to anyone but his club leadership, and even then, only when he screwed up. "Another thing, though. I want you to give him my number."

"So you can plan against me?"

Jake forced himself to take a deep breath before responding. "I can get his number elsewhere. I'm asking you to put us in touch with each other so he can let me know if your asshole ex shows up there. It would be nice to have a heads up if he's headed for us."

"Oh. I guess you have a point." She sounded disappointed, and maybe a little let down that she couldn't argue with him about it.

It reminded him of how fiery and opinionated she'd been in school. Was that because she liked to argue sometimes? Did she need a little safe conflict to feel secure? It wasn't a deal breaker for him, but he wasn't doing it over the phone, where he couldn't read her body language and where he couldn't kiss away any anger the disagreement might cause.

"You know, you make it really hard for a girl to stay pissed at you," she said.

"It's a gift." Jake couldn't help the grin that spread across his face as he imagined her rolling her eyes at his quip.

"It's something," her tone was deadpan. She let out an audible sigh. "I guess I should go. I have one more thing to add to my to do list today. You'll let me know as soon as you have an answer? How sure are you they'll agree?"

"I have little doubt I'll get the go ahead. The question is where to have you set up and if there's power. Oh when you give Iceman my number have him send me how big the trailer is too. That will give me an idea of where we can fit it."

"Alright. I guess I better get started, or I'll never be ready by morning."

"If you need an extra day to be ready, take it. I'll be here."

"No. I can do it. I've been a lump on Matt's couch for long enough. I need to do something, even if it's just something different."

"If you say so." He wasn't going to engage her now, even though he got the feeling that was what she was after.

They talked for a couple of moments longer, wrapping up plans and saying goodbyes, before they rang off.

Once off the phone, Jake went back to the common area, where most of the two chapters of the club were gathered, as it was almost lunchtime. He caught Lurch's attention and tilted the top of his head toward the barn where they kept the equipment, as it would likely be at least mostly empty this time of day.

"What's up?" Lurch asked.

Jake gave him a brief overview of what he'd learned a couple days earlier, as well as his history with Heather and what little he'd been able to learn about this Mitch since.

"I'd like to see here again. But it's not feasible for me to go up there, not now. And I don't know how long it will be until I can get away for that kind of time. But she's hiding and we think we've found a solution."

"Why does it feel like this place is becoming a sanctuary for battered women?" Lurch said with a shake of his head. "Other than that you know her from a million years ago and you want into her pants now, give me a good reason to tell you yes."

"Aside from you having a hard time turning away a woman in need? How about it will put the Kings in our debt. They've been protecting her, or else she wouldn't have been on the run. If we are keeping her here, that's another stop, another layer of people to catch and stop him before he gets to her."

"I like that element. Tell me what's her plan. We're fresh out of space, and I met her, she didn't seem like the kind to want to camp in a tent, even short term."

"She's not," Jake admitted with a grin, "but her cousin, Iceman, has a fifth wheel he's willing to let her borrow, if we'll let her park it here."

Lurch stared at him a moment. "How big?"

"I'm not sure yet." Jake checked his phone. "I take that back, it's thirty-two feet."

"So not small but not huge. I don't care if she parks it here, but you'll be responsible for her. You know how it works. Let's go check with Tuck and see if he knows about anywhere we can at least hook her up to electricity."

It took them a few minutes to find Tuck, he was in the horse barn brushing what Jake recognized as his favorite gelding. The horse he rode when he needed to go out on the ranch to do something.

Lurch explained what was going on, and asked if there was any place they could plug it in.

"Yeah. That pole out behind the bunkhouse? It has a power box for an RV on it. There's also a sewer hookup out there somewhere not too far away. Though you might have to kick around a little to find it," Tuck said.

"There's actually a hookup?" Lurch watched the ranch owner, his head tilted to one side.

"Yeah, the foreman lived in a trailer out there while your house was being built." Tuck shrugged as he continued brushing down the horse. "Might as well get some use out of it, though it might need a little work before it's usable. Do we have anyone with electrical experience?"

"I'm not sure. I'll ask around. I'm sure we'll find someone who can at least check things out," Lurch said, then turned to Jake. "How long do we have until the trailer gets here?"

"Not until tomorrow. Even if she leaves early, she likely won't be here until at least noon."

"She's already coming for sure?" Lurch asked, one brow lifted.

Jake shook his head. "She's waiting to hear from me tonight before it's a sure thing."

Lurch nodded. "Go ahead and have her come down. We'll get the hook up situation figured out. If worse comes to worse, hopefully we can at least get her power, even if she has to use the bathroom and shower in the bunkhouse."

Jake pulled out his phone and started typing out messages to both Heather and Iceman letting them know everything was a go on his end.

Heather: Great. Can't wait to see you tomorrow.

While he was reading her message, his phone buzzed in his hand with a message from Iceman. He flipped to read that.
Iceman: I'll make sure she's ready. You keep her safe once she gets there or you'll answer to me.
Jake replied to Iceman first since that would be a short message.
Jake to Iceman: 10-4
Jake to Heather: Me either, but don't rush. Take your time and drive safe.
He looked up to find both Lurch and Tuck watching him.
"What?" he asked, looking back and forth between them.
Tuck shook his head. "Just wondering how long until you noticed us watching you." He went back to brushing the horse.
"How long was it?"
"Not long," Lurch said.
"Well, we're done here, I think. Unless you have something else for me to do, I'll go check out the trailer site, see if it needs cleaning up. Maybe I can find the sewer hookup."
"At least we'll know where to find you," Lurch said before turning back to Tuck.
Jake nodded, waved one hand at them over his shoulder and left them behind as he headed to the bunkhouse. He went through the building instead of around, then stood outside the back door for a moment, scanning the area. He took in possible cover and escape routes just in case they were needed. Then once he had a mental picture of the space, he made his way over to the pole, picking his way through the scattered weeds, until beside the pole, he spotted the metal box that had to contain the power hookup.
From there he scanned the ground, trying to spot the septic hookup. He didn't see anything obvious, but there were a lot of low weeds covering the ground. Getting rid of those would probably help.

His gaze played over the area as he considered the best way to do it. A hoe would be fastest, but it would leave roots that would only grow back in a week or two. No, he would be better off doing it right from the beginning.

After retrieving a pair of gloves he got busy, and managed to pull all the weeds in a little more than an hour. Another twenty minutes and he had them gathered and tossed in the compost heap to breakdown. He was standing next to the pole with the hookup, stretching his aching back and wondering if maybe he shouldn't clear a bigger area when Steele approached.

"Hey, I hear there's some electrical box that needs to be checked out?" Steele asked once he was close enough not to need to yell.

"Yeah. You know much about electrical?" Jake asked.

Steele nodded. "Three years as an apprentice, I'm not certified, but I can do simple jobs. Is this the box?" He motioned to the box mounted three feet from the ground on the pole by where Jake stood.

"This is it. The plan is to plug an RV in if it can handle it."

"And if it can't?"

"I haven't thought that far ahead. I guess I'll have to figure something else out."

"Let me take a look before we worry about it too much." Steele went down on one knee, and lifted the lid on the box, doing something Jake didn't see to get the box to stay open. He pulled some boxy looking tool with wires and sharp points on the end out of his back pocket and started poking the ends into the outlet.

Jake took a step back. There were a lot of things he could do, or didn't mind trying, but getting fried by electricity wasn't one of them.

16

Heather cupped her left hand under the right, where it held the pistol out in front of her and sited in on the target. When she was sure she was on it, she squeezed the trigger, then repeated the process until she'd emptied the magazine.

"How many rounds do I need to put through it before you're satisfied?" she asked as she hit the release and popped out the magazine.

"At least thirty. I'd be happier with at least fifty," Matt said, handing her another magazine.

"I can reload myself," Heather said as she shoved the clip home then pulled back the slide and let it go.

"Yeah, but it's faster this way. I'll let you reload them later while I clean that." He nodded toward the pistol in her hand. "Then you can take it to Wyoming with you, and I won't have to worry quite so much about you."

"I don't mean for you to worry about me." She picked the pistol up and aimed again.

"I know you don't," Matt said after she finished emptying the second magazine at the target. He hit the button next to her to bring the paper target to them while she ejected the spent magazine. "You're doing pretty good. A nice tight grouping, except for this one over here." He pointed to one hole a couple of inches from the rest.

"That was my first shot. I was getting a feel for it." She lifted one shoulder and let it fall. "Everything after that one has been good."

He watched her for a moment, as if waiting for her to change her story or as if he doubted her and was waiting for her to break. But she wouldn't. It had been her first shot, and the pistol had kicked a little more than she'd been prepared for. After the first shot she'd had a better idea and had braced for it.

"Could you pull it if Mitch or the men he's mixed up with find you? Could you use it on a person if it meant your life?" Matt asked, one brow lifted.

"Damn. You're not pulling any punches today, are you?"

"I can't afford to. I'm getting ready to let you take off and go two states away on your own. I want to know that if something happens, you can, and will, defend yourself."

Heather laid the pistol on the counter between her and the range where she'd been shooting at the target, turned to Matt, where he stood a little behind her. And wrapped her arms around his middle. She hugged him, pressing her forehead against his chest.

"Thank you." She wanted to say more, but she couldn't force the words past the lump in her throat.

"What are you thanking me for?" His voice was gruff, but his arms went around her, holding her and letting her know that even though he was gritty, abrasive, and often not the nicest person she knew, that he cared. That he wanted her to know he cared, even if it wasn't in his nature to show it.

"For trying to take care of me. For caring. Just for being you I guess." She took a deep breath and looked up at him, propping her chin against his chest as she did. "Mostly, I think for being there when I needed you, and not fighting me when I want to do this. I know it's probably a stupid thing to do. That it's unlikely it will be more than a fling between old friends, but it means a lot to me that you're not trying to stop me or talk me out of it."

"Sweetheart," Matt looked down at her with one corner of his mouth quirked up, "I learned a long time ago not to try to get between you and whatever you've set your mind on. I'm pretty sure I still have scars from the last time I tried."

She rolled her eyes. "It wasn't that bad."

"Sweetheart, I was nearly trampled by the mustang you had decided you were going to ride."

"And I did it, didn't I?" She remembered the incident. She'd been barely fifteen and determined to do the same thing all the boys were. She'd spent the week following her brothers and cousins around, wanting to be included. The way she'd seen it, the only way to be considered one of them was to do what they were doing. And she'd refused to be talked out of it. Not by Matt, and not by her brothers, once they'd realized she was serious about climbing on that horse's back just like they had.

"You did it, but we all learned a lesson that day." His voice was serious as he leaned down and kissed her forehead. "Don't issue a challenge because we think it will scare you off. I swear you scared the shit out of me that day. But your dad nearly killed Billy and Craig."

Heather lifted one shoulder and let it fall. "They're the ones who thought it up and challenged me to do it. I just wanted to be included. And I can't say I failed."

"No, you didn't fail but when your dad stepped out of the barn and saw you on the back of that mustang, it bucking as hard as it could, I thought he was going to have a heart attack. When you managed to get off the horse without being hurt, I thought he would kill your brothers."

"He wouldn't kill them. Maybe chew them out a little, but I can't recall them getting into much trouble before that. He always seemed to think they could do no wrong."

Matt shook his head. "You were just too young to remember them getting into trouble. They got into plenty. They'd mostly calmed down by the time you were big enough to remember it."

"But you do?"

"Remember them wild? Sure do. Of course, for a lot of it, I was in the thick of it with them, so of course I'd remember it."

Heather stared up at him a moment, then spoke, "And that's why you're my favorite cousin." She pulled away and turned back to the pistol lying on the counter. "But if you tell anyone I said that I'll deny it."

Matt chuckled. "Of course you would. But I don't need to tell anyone. Knowing myself is all I need." He handed her another full magazine, then clipped a fresh target to the carrier, then sent it back into position with the press of a button. "Two more magazines and we can call it good."

Heather picked up the mag, slammed it home and took aim. It wasn't that she didn't enjoy shooting, but she had other things she needed to get done. She wanted to make sure she had everything for her trip and that she'd gathered all her things up from where they'd been scattered around Matt's house over the last couple of weeks.

Still, that he was going to loan her a weapon, and that he was taking the time to make sure she knew how to use it wasn't anything small, and she did appreciate it. Even if telling him as much would make him start to question her sanity. Well, maybe not start. She was sure she'd made more than a few decisions in the past that had already started that line of thought, but she didn't need to push anyone, especially not Matt, with all he'd done for her recently, farther in that direction.

"L ET's GRAB SOMETHING TO eat," Matt said as he turned the key in his pickup. "That way you can finish packing, and we won't have to worry about cleaning up afterwards."

"Sure. What do you have in mind?" She'd learned in the time she'd been staying with him that Matt didn't cook much. It wasn't that he couldn't but who wanted to cook for one person? She did it frequently, but it wasn't that she wanted to, or liked to. Her reason was that she got tired of nothing but eating out and fast food. Besides, her cooking tasted better. But today, with other things to do, she'd take it.

"What do you have left to do to be ready?" he asked once they were seated in what she'd discovered was his favorite diner and had given the waitress their orders.

"Not a whole lot. I want to make one last pass through the house to make sure I've gathered up all my junk. You don't need to put up with my shit in your way, especially if I'm not there."

"I'll miss having you around." He tilted his head to one side and watched her. "It's been nice having you around again. I didn't realize how much I missed being around family, and you and your brothers in particular."

Heather shook her head. "I don't know why anyone would miss those fools." She couldn't resist teasing him. "I see them way too often to suit me." Well, she had before she'd come up here.

Going to Craig had been her first thought when she'd known she had to get away from Mitch, but as soon as she'd thought it, she'd dismissed it. She couldn't endanger his family. The same with Billy. Plus, it couldn't hurt to put more distance between her and the club he'd all but sold her too. No, she couldn't put her brothers or their kid in danger. That had meant going to someone who didn't have the same entanglements, and who had what it would take to help her figure things out, at least until she figured out what to do about Mitch and those people. Maybe then it would be safe enough to go back to Alabama, if only to see her family again.

17

JAKE HAD A HARD time keeping his eyes off the road into the ranch. Heather had texted twenty minutes before, letting him know she was in Gillette and on her way. Now he was impatient to see her again. And nervous to make sure she was okay. This morning he'd finally heard back from Hex and his inquiries into what was going on in Mobile with her ex and whoever he was mixed up with.

In catching up, Jake had found out the name of the club that Hex was in down there. A club called the Savage Warriors. Once he'd found that out Jake had contacted Gizmo to see what the tech captain of the original chapter could tell him about the Warriors.

It had taken longer than he'd liked, though not as long as the information from Hex had, but Jake couldn't have been more shocked if the Warriors had been the club Heather's ex was mixed up with. Not that they were. No. It was even more shocking.

After doing some checking through channels, Giz had let him know that the Warriors were another club like the Souls. One that looked like a one percent club, but in reality, was filled with undercover agents from different agencies. After Gizmo had given him that bombshell, Jake had pulled out the burner he kept stashed just for this purpose, found a few minutes of privacy, and reached out to his handler at the DEA to verify.

Because his undercover situation wasn't like most, he and his handler didn't have the usual relationship or even regular check ins. The club as a whole did check ins with the various agencies, those were done on a regular basis, usually behind closed doors and from a secure connection. Then each brother had their own contacts, but only reached out if they needed to verify something or if there was a problem somewhere along the way.

It had taken him a few hours, but Marc had confirmed that the Warriors were another club like the Souls, that all the members, including Hex, were attached to some government entity, working to clean up the country, from the dark side of the law.

Now he knew he could trust the info from Hex, but he wondered if he should let his old buddy know what was going on, and how to do that and make sure it stayed secure. Because as much as he wanted to take care of things for Heather, he couldn't risk his brothers' lives to do it.

He rubbed the back of his neck and scanned the horizon again as he tried to figure out how to handle the thing with Hex and the Warriors, but Hex had told him what he'd been able to find out about the situation. That Mitch owed a club some serious money. Word on the street was he'd been dealing for a club and had come up short. No one was sure if he was using from the supply, he'd been robbed or just given it away, but he owed a quarter of million dollars.

From what Hex had been able to find out, he'd offered to pay the debt by giving the Wandering Sons, which was the club he'd been selling for, Heather, as the president had a thing for her. The Sons' president had agreed, but only to let her cover the interest, but before the exchange could be made, Heather had disappeared. Now both the club and Mitch were looking for her, though from what Hex had said, the Sons didn't seem all that invested. From what he'd said, they'd take an interest if she was in the area, but they weren't searching the country for her.

That cocksucker she'd been living with was a different story. Hex said Coleman had called her family and everyone they'd known searching for her, no one seemed to know where she was, or if they did, they weren't telling him. The longer she was gone, the more desperate he became. Jake had no doubt it was in no small part because every day his debt increased.

Jake took a deep breath and pushed the thoughts of Heather's ex and the trouble he'd gotten himself into out of his mind. He scanned the horizon again. A wave of relief washed through him when he spotted the plume of dust on the road from the highway. She was here.

He headed out to intercept her before she pulled the truck into the driveway. It would be easier if they pulled the trailer back here to begin with, rather than have to jockey it around to get it where it needed to go later.

"Hey, I wasn't expecting you to be waiting on me," Heather said through her open window after easing the truck to a stop in front of where he stood on one side of the road.

"I thought it would be easier to pull the trailer into it's space as you pulled in, rather than move it later, after you'd pulled all the way into the yard."

"Sounds good. Where you want it?"

"Over behind the bunkhouse. You want me to drive it back there or hop into the passenger seat to give you directions?"

"Passenger's seat is fine," she said, hitting the lock button on the door.

Jake went around the front of the truck and slid into the passenger seat. Before she put the truck back in gear, he leaned over the middle seat, which was folded down to look more like a console than a seat. "I'm glad to see you made it safe." She turned toward him and before she had a chance to realize what he was doing, or stop him, not that he thought she would, he dropped a brief, chaste kiss on her lips, then settled into his seat. "You're going to want to take the right fork over here. We're going to stay on that side of all the buildings."

Heather stared at him for a moment, and he wasn't sure if it was surprise, or if she had something she wanted to say. Either way, she didn't say anything but put the truck in gear and followed his directions.

18

Heather blinked several times, wondering if she should say something about the kiss Aaron had planted on her, as if it was something they'd always done. She stared at him for a few seconds then decided she wasn't sure what she wanted to say, not yet. So she put the truck in gear and followed his directions.

Thirty minutes later, she'd parked the trailer and working together, they'd managed to get it hooked up to both power and sewer, now she just had to finish with the set up and get it leveled. Thankfully, the spot he'd had her park in looked pretty level already. She had been surprised when he'd told her there was a sewer hookup so she wouldn't need to rely on the bunkhouse bathroom, but she wasn't sure how much she'd use the trailer for that anyway. Bathrooms in trailers tended to be small and cramped. Still, she'd figure it out as they went along.

"What else needs to be done?" Aaron asked, as he stood to one side, hands on his hips as he looked from one end of the trailer to the other.

"We need to drop the jacks and level it. I can do it if you've got something else to do."

"No, Lynnie, I'm yours all afternoon, unless something big comes up, and there's no reason to think anything will."

"Thanks." She couldn't help the warmth that spread through her at the idea. She went to the storage box and pulled out the cordless drill and fitting Matt had told her were for the jacks, as well as the level that would sit on the tongue.

"Here, let me help." Aaron took the drill and went around the trailer, running each one until it hit the ground. "What needs more lift?" He stood on the other side of the tongue from where she stood.

"Let me see." She set the small level on the tongue and waited a moment for the air bubble to settle. Another ten minutes of her shouting directions and Aaron working the jacks and they had the trailer all set. He put away the drill while she went inside and opened up the slides. She stood in the doorway looking around, thinking she could stay in here a lot more than the few days she had planned, if she needed to. Hell, this might be bigger than her first apartment, and it was a hell of a lot nicer. Aaron came up the stairs behind her, she didn't move, knowing there was enough space for him to step up inside, and she wasn't through taking the place in.

"What do you think, Lynnie? Is it doable?" Aaron came up behind her, his hands settled on her hips, and she felt his jaw alongside her ear as he spoke softly.

"I was just thinking about how nice it is. I think it's bigger than my first apartment."

"I know it's more space than I have inside," he said, "and it's all yours."

"I'd be willing to share if you need some space." She couldn't help the grin that made its way across her face as she continued, "I think the couch makes out into a bed." She wanted to turn and look at him, to gauge his reaction, but she didn't want to move from where she was now. She liked having his hands on her. Besides, they were just starting to get to know each other again. It was too soon to invite him to share her bed. Yet.

"Lynnie," his voice had dropped to a low rumble that made her stomach flip and heat pool low in her belly. "If I'm sharing this place with you, I'm not going to be sleeping on the couch."

She let her head drop, trying to figure out how to tell him she wasn't ready for that, not yet. It was too soon. Not because she'd only gotten away from Mitch a couple of weeks ago, but because she didn't know him that well, not anymore. Yes, she'd come to spend a few days with him, but that was because he had things going on and couldn't come up to see her. The distance was just too much with what he had going on in his life. She had nothing tying her to Dickenson, so it worked for her to come closer to him. Still, that didn't mean she was ready to jump in to bed with him.

"Relax, Lynnie. I'm not pushing. I just wanted to let you know I'm not playing games here. I am and have always been serious about you."

That caught her attention. She turned to face him, the hands he'd set on her hips sliding as she moved, sending flutters of anticipation through her.

"Always?"

"As long as I can remember." Aaron's voice was little more than a whisper, but it didn't need to be more. She heard him just fine.

Her heart fluttered in her chest. "But you never said anything back then." She wished he had. She would have gone out with him in a heartbeat.

"As I told you on the phone the other day, I was a chicken, and about the time I built up enough guts to ask, I found out we were leaving. Then I didn't ask on purpose. I didn't want to start something only to have to leave."

Heather lifted one hand to cup his cheek as she gazed up at him. "I wish you'd asked. I would have taken whatever time we had together."

His hands slid from her hips, around to her back and he tugged her closer, until the fronts of their bodies just brushed each other. "I wanted to. And I've wished several times over the years that I had, but now I think it just wasn't our time.

If we'd dated then, then had a rough break up because of the distance, it would have ruined our chances now."

"I like the now." She found herself leaning closer, wishing he'd kiss her again. This time it wouldn't be the chaste brush of lips he'd given her earlier.

"Me too."

He leaned close and brushed her lips with his, so gently she might have imagined it, but she wasn't about to let that be all. The hand on his cheek slid around to the back of his neck and she tugged him closer as she opened her mouth beneath his.

Aaron didn't hesitate, his arms tightened around her, and his mouth crushed against hers, the kiss turning hot and needy instead of the chaste thing he'd tried to give her. And Heather didn't hesitate to give as good as she got. Her nipples tightened and her entire body heated as she melted against him, letting her body tell him exactly what she wanted.

19

Jake hadn't planned to take things this far, at least not this fast but when he'd brushed a gentle kiss across her lips, Heather had opened up to him, snapping the thin cord of control he'd had on his need to taste her. As the kiss deepened, she melted against him, letting him feel how well her body fit against his. His hand came up and cupped her cheek as his tongue tasted every inch of her mouth.

His cock ached and a growl escaped his throat as he forced himself to lift his head and break the kiss. "Damn, Lynnie, you do things to me. Things I know better than to do, but somehow, I just can't help myself." He pressed his forehead against hers, unable to move his hand from her face.

"You started it."

Her words might have been teasing, but her voice was low and husky and made him want to pick her up, find the bed, strip her naked and spend a week or five worshipping her body. But now wasn't the time. Not with two clubs outside waiting for him to bring her out and make introductions.

"I want to start a lot more, but now's not the time. You want to unpack things in here and take a few to unwind from the trip or you ready to meet everyone?"

Her eyes went wide. "There's more than were in Sturgis the other day?"

"Only a couple, but I figured there were a lot of people and a lot of new faces. You probably don't remember everyone, and I know they likely won't, so why not refresh everyone's memories?"

She leaned back so their heads were no longer pressed together and blinked several times as if trying to focus on his face.

Jake picked his head up and watched her.

"That's sweet." She took a deep breath and looked around "Can I get ten minutes to freshen up and wash off a little of the road dust? Then I'll be ready to go meet everyone."

"Sure thing. Can I get you something to drink?"

"What do you have?"

"Water, sodas, beer, most of the hard liquors, mixers, pretty much anything you want. The girls even have a blender set up for frozen drinks."

"Really?"

"This isn't normal. We've kind of had a running party for that last week or so while the charter chapter is visiting. I'm not saying we don't drink and get a little wild but not usually to this degree."

"I'll take a beer then," she said with a shrug, before turning toward the front of the trailer.

"What kind?"

"Whatever you have."

"We have a bunch, what do you normally drink?"

"I'll drink Shiner, Amber Bock, Dos Equis, Phat Fish, that kind of thing. Does that help?" She stopped a few steps away and twisted around to look at him.

"It does. I'll go grab you something. Want me to knock when I come back or come on in?"

"Just come on in. I'll probably be in the bedroom or the bathroom." She turned and continued on.

He watched as she disappeared through a doorway, then turned and stepped down from the trailer. Shaking his head at how easily she'd changed what he'd intended to be a quick, gentle kiss into something far more intense.

"You going to disappear now that your girl's here?" Dumbass asked as Jake dug through a cooler looking for a good beer for her.

"Nah." Jake didn't bother looking up. "I'm grabbing us something to drink while she washes up a little. It's a long drive. Then we'll come out and she can meet everyone."

"Didn't she meet people a few days ago?"

Jake pulled two bottles from the icy water and set them on top of another cooler before glancing up at his friend.

"Some, but I don't know about all. Plus there were a lot of people there. Do you remember everyone you met that day?"

"Hell no," Dumbass said with a chuckle.

"Exactly. So we'll re-introduce her. If she's only here for a day or two, no harm no foul, but if she's here longer, it will pay off in the end."

"Only a day or so. She drove all this way and brought a trailer for a day or two?"

Jake shrugged. "We didn't really set a time on it. We wanted to see each other again, and it was too far for me to go right now. I didn't want her spending money on a motel room, and I don't have a place for her to stay, so she found an alternative. As for how long, if I have my way, it will be a lot more than a day or two." He didn't say that was only partly because it gave her another layer of protection from the ex, that as far as he'd been able to tell, was still looking for her. Even if she could be traced to Iceman, there was no reason to come here, nothing to tie her to him, at least not in the last ten plus years. Hopefully, even if they did trace her to North Dakota then down here, Iceman would be able to give them a head's up. "We'll be back in a few." He carried the drinks back around to the rear of the bunkhouse to her trailer, and let himself in.

"I'm back," he called out.

"Have a seat, I'll be right out," Heather called back.

Jake looked around, paying attention to the place for the first time. Before, he'd been more focused on her. Now, he spotted the sofa, and considered sitting there, but opted for the table, and the bench seat on one side, as he could set down the beer instead of letting it grow warm from the heat of his hands.

Taking a seat, he twisted the top off his bottle and took a pull while he waited for Heather. This place was nicer than he'd anticipated. When she'd said trailer, he had pictured the little camp trailer that his dad had borrowed from his grandparents when he was a teenager, it had looked like something straight out of the sixties. Including the old fashion, cracking upholstery, and floral chintz curtains. This was spacious and far more modern looking, almost like a real home.

"That feels so much better," Heather said stepping down off a set of stairs Jake hadn't noticed into the main room of the trailer. He looked over to find that she'd changed into a pair of shorts and a tank top, from the jeans and hoodie she'd been wearing earlier. His guess was that it had been cool when she'd pulled out of Dickenson that morning. She'd also brushed out her hair and pulled it up into a ponytail. And from the slight pink tint to her face, he guessed she'd washed her face too. The whole look made him want to pick her up, haul her back into the bedroom and show her exactly what she did to him. But they hadn't gotten that far. No yet. But soon, he hoped.

"You look great." He knew enough about women to know better than to tell her she looked better than before, that would only start a line of questions he didn't want to get into. What was wrong with how she'd looked before? Nothing, but she looked like she felt better now. Still, he didn't want to get into it.

"Thanks. I still have a little unloading/unpacking to do but it can wait. Let's go meet your friends. Is that mine?" she motioned to the bottle on the table beside him.

"Yep, here." He picked it up and twisted the top off before handing it to her.

"Thanks." She took it, and he couldn't keep from watching as she tipped the bottle back, exposing the long length of her throat.

Jake tightened his grip on his own bottle, resisting the urge to reach up and stroke that skin to see if it was as soft as it looked.

"Well, are we going out to see everyone?" Heather asked as she lowered the bottle.

"Sure, let's go." Jake stood, motioned for her to lead the way out, then tried to subtly adjust his jeans where they'd suddenly grown much tighter than they'd been just moments before.

"Should I lock it?" She stopped at the foot of the steps up into the trailer and asked as he descended the same stairs.

"You can if you want, but no one will bother it. We also won't be offended if you feel like you should," he said.

Heather tilted her head and watched him. "How about I don't if we're on the ranch. I can lock it if we leave for some reason. And at night."

"Whatever you want to do." He wondered why she planned to lock it at night, but didn't ask, not yet. He'd wait for a better time to ask that.

20

Heather followed Aaron through the door at the building in front of where he'd had her park her borrowed trailer.

"This is the restroom, and the showers," he motioned off to one side as they came in. "They're communal showers, so we've got a schedule right now for men and women's shower time. If you're still around after the Tucson bunch leaves, we'll work something out if you want to use these instead of the shower in the trailer. You're welcome to do either." He continued through the building. "The kitchen, when we don't have a big group, lunches are available in here, breakfast and dinner are served at the big house. Through there," he motioned toward a doorway at the far end of the large room, "are the bunks. And we've got the TV in here, it's got streaming TV and a PS5. There's usually a couple of guys playing in the evenings, but you'll probably have open access during the day while most of us are busy."

Heather looked around and took in the space. It was cleaner than she'd expected for a space lived in and maintained by a bunch of men. It made her wonder if maybe more than just Aaron was previously military? She wanted to ask if she could see the bunk rooms, but thought maybe that was going too far. Maybe later if things worked out.

"And out here is where we're all gathering." He led her through the doorway and out into what looked like a large driveway that had been converted into a gathering area with several picnic tables on one side, a large firepit near the center surrounded with more chairs than she cared to count at the moment, and what looked like an outdoor kitchen set up on the side opposite the tables. "Meals, for now are served over there. There are also coolers with drinks of all kind under the tables. Help yourself. You're welcome at all meals, now and after our visitors leave, or no one will hold it against you if you want to cook for yourself or go into town. I would appreciate it if you let me know if you're going to leave the ranch. It's not that I want to limit your movements, or restrict you in anyway, but until we know what's up with Mitch and the assholes that he's running with, I just want to make sure you're safe."

She scanned the area, taking in all the faces, some familiar, some she didn't recall having seen, and only paying a little attention to what Aaron was saying. She nodded as he stopped speaking, barely registering what he was saying as she thought about meeting all these people, what would they think of her and how would she keep everyone's names straight?

"Hi!" A woman's voice beside her drew Heather back to what was going on. She blinked and turned to find the woman beside her smiling and looking friendly. "I'm Robyn. We met the other day, but you may not remember me. There were a lot of people, and I know I don't remember half the people I met."

"I do remember you; we didn't talk much but I remember you were with Ghost, right?"

"I am, how did you remember that with all the new names and faces?"

"Ghost was one of those that hit something in my memory, and I couldn't forget it. It reminded me of an old movie I saw when I was a teenager. And it just clicked."

"Ohh. What was the movie? I might have to see it. He reminded you of it, you say?"

"Well, it wasn't that he reminded me, it was more that his name did. The name of the movie is The Ghost and The Darkness. It was about hunting men killing lions in Africa. I heard it was based on a true story, but I'm not sure if that's true or not."

"Now that you tell me a little about it, I think I have heard of it, though I don't think I've seen it. Why don't you come over here and we can get to know each other a little better?" Robyn tilted her head toward a group of women sitting in a bunch of chairs clustered in the shade. They looked happy and friendly. Heather wanted to join them, but she wasn't ready to leave Aaron.

"Aaron was just showing me around and making sure I know everyone. How about I join you when we're done making the rounds?"

"That would be great. Let him introduce you to the guys, then we'll take care of the women and all the details you need to know to hang around a group like this."

"Sounds great. I'm sure I'll join you soon."

Robyn waved, turned toward the kitchen area, dug something out of one of the coolers, then went back to where the other women sat. There looked like there was six to eight there and Heather wasn't sure, but it seemed there were some missing.

"Ready?" Aaron's voice brought her attention back to him.

She turned and looked up at him with a smile. "Sure. Let's go."

They spent the next forty-five minutes meeting and talking to different men. She still wasn't sure how she would remember who everyone was, much less their names. Though for some reason she thought their nicknames would stick with her better than real names would have, similar to how she had an easier time remembering pets' names than people's. Things like Malice and Savage seemed to stand out in her mind.

"Why do they call you Jake?"

"It's a nickname, just like Ghost, Lurch, and the others."

"I know that, but why? There's always a reason behind a nickname and I want to know yours." She watched his reaction and noticed how his face turned pink.

"It's dumb. You don't need to know."

"Need to? No. But I want to and the more you resist telling me, the more I want to know. The more I'm going to pester you about it. You and I both know you might as well just tell me. Cause I won't let up until I find out… or I could just go ask someone else." She twisted around to look toward the group of men they'd just walked away from. "Sadist seems like the kind who would tell me just to get a rise out of you."

Aaron pinched the bridge of his nose. "Jesus. Why are you like this?"

Heather shrugged. "I don't know. I'm just me. That's all I can be."

"And honestly, I wouldn't want you any other way." He hooked an arm around her waist and tugged her close as he took a deep breath and heaved out a sigh. "I'll tell you, but it's embarrassing."

She wanted to stop and look at him, to watch his face as he told her but knew that would only make him more self-conscious.

"When I was in my first duty assignment after basic there was another guy with the same last name. There was some discussion as to how to tell us apart, when some smart ass pipped up and told them they should call me Jake because I looked like the guy from those stupid insurance commercials. It stuck."

Heather started by giggling. She remembered those commercials. Not the newer versions, but the original. And now that she thought about it, he did look a little like the actor when he'd been younger. Not so much now that he'd lost some of the baby fat and put on some muscle. "He wasn't wrong." She glanced up at Aaron and found the scowl on his face even funnier than the reason behind his nickname. The giggles became full blown laughter. Not at his nickname or how he came by it, but at his reaction to her.

He put his hands on his hips and watched as she laughed, and Heather found that even funnier. She gasped for air, knowing this wasn't as funny as she thought it was. Maybe it was more than the story he'd told her? She liked the way he made her feel safe, cared for but free at the same time.

She wiped tears from the corners of her eyes as she gasped for air, the laughter finally subsiding. "Thanks, I needed that."

"Glad I could help, even if it was only by being the butt of the joke."

"It wasn't that. Not the way you think. It was your reaction, the look on your face. That was what was so funny."

He shook his head at her, a smile slowly creeping onto his face. "You know, it's a good thing I like you."

"I guess I kind of like you too."

He held a hand out toward her, and without thinking about it she took it in hers, weaving her fingers in with his as she let him pull her along to the next person he wanted her to meet.

21

Jake didn't know how he found her laughter so amusing, especially when it was him she was laughing at, but oddly he didn't mind. He just liked that she felt safe enough to laugh like that. Maybe that was part of what had caused it, the need to let off some steam. He hoped she never felt like she couldn't be herself around him.

Once she'd finished laughing and was ready to meet the rest of the crew, he held out a hand, only realizing once he'd done it that maybe she wouldn't be comfortable with it, but to his surprise, she took it. She wove her fingers in between his and held on. Unable to wipe the stupid grin off his face, one he knew he'd take some ribbing for later, he took her to meet the others.

By the time she'd met the guys gathered around the firepit and outdoor kitchen, her eyes had glazed over, and he could tell they'd surpassed her ability to remember names, but she remained friendly and cheerful.

"I'm going to take mercy on you, and call it good for now. We'll worry about meeting the rest of the guys later."

She looked at him with wide eyes, with just a little panic on her face. "There are more?"

"Yeah," he said with a chuckle. "But they're off doing something, either somewhere on the ranch or in town. You can meet them as they come in." He glanced down at the beer bottle in her hand. "Want another?" He motioned toward it with his own bottle.

"That would be great. Where do I get them?"

"They're in the coolers over there." He tilted his head toward the outdoor kitchen. "But go sit down with the women, I'll bring it to you."

"Are you sure? You don't have to wait on me."

"I don't mind." Jake reluctantly let go of her hand, took her empty bottle, then watched as she made her way toward where the women sat in the shade, waiting until she spoke to one of them, found a chair and sat before turning away. After dropping the empties in the recycling bin, he pulled out two fresh drinks, delivered Heather's to her, then went to join the men.

Mac stared at him for several seconds, then made a show of turning to look at Heather, and watching her for a few moments before looking back to Jake. This went on for several minutes, Jake doing his best to ignore it until Sadist spoke up.

"Just spit it out, man. You're going to hurt yourself trying to keep it in as you wait for him to ask."

"Well, she's not carrying a purse, so I'm just wondering where she keeps them," Mac said, still looking back and forth between Heather and Jake.

Jake rolled his eyes. He might as well get it over with. Mac wouldn't be happy until he got it out.

"Where she keeps what?" Jake asked, knowing he deserved this. He'd done his share of ribbing each of the others as they'd met their women. At least they were doing it when she wasn't present. He wasn't sure yet how she would take the kind of ribbing his brothers tended to dish out. Though after the way she'd laughed earlier, maybe she would do okay.

"Your balls. Because the way you were leading her around, making sure she met everyone then fetching a drink and serving it to her like some kind of princess, I'm sure she's got possession of them now."

The men around them cracked up and even Jake smiled as he shook his head. "Maybe so, but if Elyse asked for a drink or even for you to fix her a plate come dinner time, you sure as hell would be up getting it for her, wouldn't you."

"Hey, I never said I wasn't whipped. I thought we established that some time ago. We were talking about you for a change."

Jake rolled his eyes. There was no point in arguing or fighting it. Talking back or trying to set them straight would only make it worse, not that he had anything to set them straight on. She didn't carry around his balls, those were still firmly in his jeans. And not happy about it at the moment, from the feel of them. They wanted to take Heather back to her trailer and continue what they'd only barely started with that kiss.

But that was moving too fast, so he pushed the thought out of his mind, told his cock to calm the fuck down and focused on what was going on around him. Not the ribbing his brothers were trying to give him, that he wouldn't rise to, but everything else.

"No more trouble from Donna's ex?" Jake didn't know what all was going on there, only that Savage had picked her up on the ride up and that she had an ex who was looking for her, and had gone as far as to follow her onto the ranch after someone had spotted her in Gillette a few days ago.

"Nothing new," Savage said from where he sat on the far side of the cold firepit. "We're still waiting to hear back from Gizmo about whether or not she'll have to divorce his ass, but we'll figure that out, and if we have to, we'll start the procedure as soon as we get back to Arizona."

"You're really going to move her to Tucson and in with you?" Jake asked.

Savage stared at him; one brow lifted. "You really think you're in a position to judge us about that right now?" He shot a pointed look toward the bunkhouse, and Jake knew, the trailer that sat on the far side.

"Hey, I'm not judging." Jake held his hands out in front of him, as if proving he wasn't armed. Things between him and Heather were different, at least in his mind. They'd known each other before and had only recently encountered each other again. In his mind, that was at least a foundation. "I was just asking."

Savage didn't reply, but watched him, with a look that said just wait, he would learn the hard way. Jake didn't want to get into it.

22

Heather couldn't help how surprised she was by how welcoming the women were. She remembered several faces from the run to Sturgis, but only a couple of names. She remembered Kerry, London, and Robyn who she'd met again earlier, but that was about it.

"Tell me more about Tucson and living in the desert," London said.

Several women took turns telling her about the heat, but it was dry. The monsoons, rain and lightning storms that should be hitting the area soon. They told her it was pretty, but not the kind of pretty she was used to.

From what Heather had been able to tell from the conversation, London was getting ready to move to Tucson, even though she'd never been there. Heather wasn't sure why she was making the move, but found the discussion fascinating anyway.

"What about you, Heather? Have you ever been to the desert?" Kerry asked after a bit, likely realizing she hadn't said anything in a while.

"Nope, sorry. I haven't even been to Vegas. I know that's not Arizona, but I hear it's pretty close, weather wise. Wish I could help though." She lifted one shoulder then let it fall.

"You might make it down, though. At least to Tucson. I hear Jake still owns his house, so he'll eventually need to go down and take care of it.

Heather nodded slowly, not saying anything. Just because he owned a house there didn't mean he would be taking her. Her coming here was so they could see if there was anything more than an old attraction between them. It didn't mean they were an item, not now or that they would last. Even if she did have hopes. Not that she would ever express them out loud. Not only would that be too embarrassing, but she might jinx herself.

"I'm sorry. We're leaving you out," Kerry said. "We should change the subject."

"Not at all," Heather said with a smile. "I'm learning things, and I'm still recovering from my trip. Don't worry about me. I'll put something in as I have something to say or I'll go get another drink," she lifted her half-full bottle, "or even go see what Aaron and the guys are talking about."

"Oh, I can give you a good idea of what they're talking about," one of the women said. Heather wasn't sure of her name. "I'm Beth by the way. Sadist is mine."

Heather looked over to where the men gathered, trying to remember which one was Sadist.

"The blond with the —?" She motioned over her head with one hand, hoping the other woman would understand she meant his wide mohawk cut that reminded her of one of the TV shows about Vikings.

"Yep, that's him."

"What are they talking about?" Heather kept her eyes on the men, watching as they spoke, some waving their hands around as they spoke, others sitting nearly motionless.

"They're giving Jake shit."

"Why?" Heather frowned and turned to look at Beth, not understanding why Aaron's friends would do that to him.

"A couple of reasons, number one being that that's the way men are, they're always giving someone shit. But the real reason is payback. He deserves it after the way he gave each of the men shit when they started bringing us around." She used a finger in the air, spun in a circle to indicate all the women around the group. "While I do feel a little sorry for him, he earned it. Most of them will keep it just among them men, he didn't have the same consideration with everyone."

Heather felt her mouth fall open as she turned back to watch them men. Had Aaron been that rude? While she didn't doubt these women's word, somehow it didn't fit the impression she had of him. Neither from when they'd been in school or this time around. He'd seemed too sweet, too nice.

"He did that?" she asked, still trying to reconcile what they were telling her with the Aaron she knew. Had the years changed him so much?

"He did. But I don't think he did it maliciously," Beth said, looking around the group, as if checking with the other women to see what they thought. "I think he either didn't think about how it might make one of us feel or didn't realize we were there or could hear him. He's a nice guy, he just sometimes lets his mouth get ahead of his brain."

"That much hasn't changed," Heather admitted.

He'd been that way in school too, often blurting out whatever popped into his head, whether it was appropriate, the right time, or not. But as irritating as that trait could be, it was also endearing. It made him more human, a little more approachable. Especially to someone like herself who knew she had baggage. Who would want to take on the shitshow that her life had become, what with Mitch and the assholes he'd apparently traded her to.

Conversation turned to the trip planned the next day. Heather knew there was something, it was part of why she'd chosen to come today instead of waiting, but she hadn't known what, exactly. As they talked, she listened, wondering what Aaron had planned for her, she knew he was planning to go, but would he want her along? She hadn't talked to him about it. If not, what would she do here? Maybe go into town, though she didn't know what she'd do there. For some reason, the thought of going into town alone, especially when Aaron would be so far away, didn't sit well with her. She'd have to talk to him tonight and see what the plan was. In the meantime, she listened in on what the women were talking about, so at least she'd have an idea what was going on.

23

That evening, after dinner had been served, and cleaned up, they sat in groups around a couple of fire pits, talking, when Jake saw Heather get up, drop her empty cup in the trash and head into the bunkhouse. He assumed she was headed for the bathroom, but when she didn't come back after a few minutes, he went looking for her.

"Heather?" he called as he stepped inside the bunkhouse.

"She went out the back door," Talon said without looking away from the TV screen where he was controlling a car as it raced through the streets.

"Thanks." He went out the back and noticed she'd turned on a couple of lights inside the trailer. From the shadow moving around inside, she hadn't yet gone to bed. Good. He wanted a chance to talk to her and hadn't had much of a chance with people around them all afternoon.

He went to the trailer and knocked on the door. He heard her moving around inside, then the door opened, swinging out over the stairs, and making him glad he hadn't climbed them to knock.

"Hey." She pushed the door open and stepped back. Jake stared at her a moment, not sure if she was inviting him in or what was going on.

"You disappeared. I got worried."

"I needed some time to myself. I'll go back out if they're still there when I'm feeling better."

"I can go if you want to be alone."

"No. You're okay. I just needed some space from all the other people. Come on in." She turned and stepped farther into the trailer. Not seeing what else to do, he stepped up inside, closing the door behind himself. Most of the noise from the gathering was shut out, not completely silencing the loud music and low murmur of people talking but significantly muffling it. He was surprised by how much quieter it was in here.

"Are you okay?" He watched as she went over to the sofa and sat.

"Yeah, I just needed some time. I'm glad you followed me. I wanted to talk to you, but didn't want to take you away from the others." She patted the seat beside her, inviting him to join her.

"I wanted to talk to you too," he said, moving to the sofa and sitting, "but I didn't want to pull you away if you were having fun."

"I'm always open to you pulling me away." She leaned over and dropped her head on his shoulder.

He noticed that sometime between when she'd come out here and he'd knocked on her door, she'd kicked off her shoes and now sat here barefoot, her toenails were painted a deep purple that oddly, he found endearing.

"I'm here for you, and while it's nice that the other women are friendly, they're not you."

"That's sweet. Did you have a good time today?" He wanted to lift his arm and wrap it around her, but wasn't sure how she'd take it, so he sat there, letting her rest her head against his shoulder, trying to watch her despite the awkward positioning.

"I did. But its been a long day, between the drive, setting up then all the stuff here. I just needed to get away for a bit."

"No worries. There's no problem with that. I did want to check with you about tomorrow though."

"I know there's some kind of trip tomorrow. The women were excited, but I never caught where you are going."

"We're going to Rushmore. I wanted to invite you along if you want to go. But if you're too tired, I don't want you feeling like you have to."

She sat up, turned sideways on the sofa so she faced him, folding her legs in front of her on the seat. "Invite me how?" She wiggled until she was more comfortable.

Jake twisted to face her, pulling one leg up into the seat, but staying careful to keep his boot off the upholstery.

"I want you to come. I think it would be fun, but I don't want you to feel like you have to," he said, watching her face, trying to figure out what she was thinking.

"I've never been to Rushmore. I'd like to see it, but I want to know more about the trip? I've only gone on the one trip with a group of bikers, that's where I ran into you. Somehow, I think that's not typical of your usual ride."

"It's not. First, every club does rides a little different. Each has their own traditions and things they do, so a typical ride with the Kings wouldn't be the same as a typical ride with the Souls. The ride to Sturgis was a special thing in that we were meeting up with the Kings. We're not doing that this time. We also don't typically bring along a grill and enough food for an army like it seems they do."

"So if you don't take food, what do you do?"

"I didn't say we don't take food. Just that we don't take a grill, especially not one big enough to be it's own trailer, though now that Lurch has seen that, we may get one. It was a nice setup and could be used on the ranch too. But food is sometimes taken, and sometimes a planned stop along the way, depending on how we're doing it, and if someone wants to take cars instead of their bike. Tomorrow the plan is to stop in Custer on our way back."

"How would I ride along? I don't have a bike and after today, I don't want to drive all day again, even if I'm not towing."

He watched her for a moment, trying to figure out what was going on in her head. Was she deliberately missing his meaning when he invited her along? He reached out, covering her hands where they sat on her lap, fidgeting with each other.

"Lynnie, when I say I'd like you to go on the ride with me tomorrow, I mean I want you with me. I want you on the back of my bike."

Slowly, she lifted her gaze until it met his. "You do?" Her voice was soft, as if she wasn't sure if she should believe him. "I know that's a big deal. I mean yeah, I rode with Matt, but he's family and that's different."

"How big of deal it is varies by the club, and even by the guy. I won't lie to you and say I've never had a woman on the back of my bike, but I've never taken one on a run. But I want you there."

Her eyes went wide. "Never?"

"Never, Lynnie." He squeezed her hands, hoping she would understand what he was trying to get across without his having to come out and say it. He hated talking about his feelings. What man didn't?

"You're sure you want it to be me?"

Jake took a deep breath and searched for the right words. He needed to do this right, so she understood how much she meant to him. Yeah, they'd only recently encountered each other again, but she had always been the one for him. The one he thought about when things got tough. The one he'd always wondered what if about. The one he'd always regretted never making a move on. But now was his chance not to regret it again.

"I want it to be you. I've always wanted it to be you, even when I didn't know if I would ever see you again." He let his gaze drop to where his hand still covered his and told her about the thoughts that had been haunting him for some time. "Sometimes I wish I'd asked you out way back then, even knowing we would be leaving. It would have been hard leaving, but then I would have known if you felt the same way I did and not been left wondering for the last twelve years."

"I wish you had too." Heather's voice was little more than a whisper, but he heard it.

He looked up to find her watching him, liquid pooling in her eyes. "As much as I think it might have been better if I'd done that, I know better. I know that if I'd asked then, we wouldn't be the same people we are now. Who knows if we would have lasted back then. I don't know that I had the experiences to recognize the best thing that's ever happened to me. What I do know is that now that I've found you again, I don't want to waste another minute, Lynnie." He lifted his free hand to cup her jaw.

"Me either." She leaned close, her gaze flicking down his face, then back to his eyes.

Jake knew what she was looking at. He wanted the same thing, but he wasn't going to push her before she was ready. Slowly, he leaned forward, giving her time to back away or tell him to stop if this wasn't what she wanted.

24

Heather's heart thundered in her ears. Was she hearing what she thought she was hearing? He'd always thought about her just as she'd dreamed about him? Her chest ached at the idea of the years they'd missed out on. But if they'd gotten together then, would it have worked? She wasn't the same person now she'd been then, and that was a good thing, at least in her opinion. Would things work between them? Even with how badly she wanted it to? The only way to find out was to jump in and try it. If she backed away now, she would always wonder, always wish she'd taken the risk. The last twelve years had taught her that.

She leaned in, closing the distance between herself and Aaron, until her lips met his. His kiss was hesitant at first, but it soon turned hungry. She met him at every turn, pouring the need and want she felt into the kiss.

As if of their own volition, her arms wrapped around his neck, pulling him closer. Sensations and emotion overwhelmed her until she barely noticed when she was scooped off the sofa and set on his lap. Though the change of surface, she noticed. Gone was the soft padding underneath her, as it was replaced with the hard warmth of his leg and a ridge she couldn't ignore and didn't want to.

Without thinking about it, her body arched against his, grinding her needy core against the hard length of him and sending waves of pleasure through her. She lost track of time, of the world around them, of everything but the two of them as she let her hands play up and down his torso while she lost herself in his taste and the feel of him beneath her.

"Are you sure?" he asked as she tugged his shirt off over his head.

"I've never been more sure. But not here. Let's go to the bedroom." Her voice had gone breathy, needy. She tried to climb off his lap, only to be stopped by his hands on her hips.

Before she could say anything, he stood, taking her with him. She let out a startled eep and wrapped her arms around his neck as he carried her through the trailer. Not used to being carried or the odd sensations it caused low in her belly, she buried her face in his neck, thankful the place wasn't big enough he would need directions.

"I hate letting go of you, Lynnie, but I can't get my boots off while holding on to you." He set her gently on the bed, then stepped back and bent to untie and loosen the laces on his boots.

She tilted sideways, until she rested on one elbow and watched the muscles in his arms and shoulders play beneath the skin as he worked his boots off. The tattoos on his arms and neck had been impossible to miss, but she should have realized his back and chest would have them too. Her fingers itched to trace the lines and colors along his skin. She couldn't help but wonder what designs his jeans hid. Hopefully, she wouldn't have too long to wait to find out.

When he'd finished with his boots, he looked up at her, a predatory look in his eye. If she wasn't so certain he would never hurt her, it might have scared her. But there were only a few people on earth she was as sure of as Aaron, though she couldn't have said why, and at the moment she didn't want to examine it.

He moved to the edge of the bed, staring down at her with hungry eyes as she lay on one side, looking up at him and hoping she looked alluring.

"Lynnie, I've wanted this for a long time, but I know you're not coming from a good place. The last thing I want is to scare you or hurt you. You can stop this at any time. If I do anything you don't like or don't want, just say something. Okay, sweetheart?"

She nodded, not entirely sure why he felt he would scare or hurt her. Yeah, she'd run from her ex and his friends, but not because they'd hurt her. She'd run before they'd had a chance.

"I need the words, Lynnie."

"I understand. If there's anything I don't want, say something."

"Good girl."

She liked hearing that. Heat pooled low in her belly, and she didn't entirely understand why, but she wasn't going to examine it, at least not yet. Leaning up, she reached for him, wrapping an arm around his neck she tugged him closer. She wanted to kiss him, to feel his mouth on hers and his hands on her skin.

His hand skimmed along her belly, over her shirt, reminding her that she was still fully dressed while she'd taken off his shirt. She didn't like that. She wanted to feel him, skin to skin. Her hands went to the bottom of her shirt and began tugging it up, working it up until she broke their kiss with a gasp, then shoved her shirt up over her head and off.

Aaron's eyes played down her body, then back up.

"You're beautiful," he said once his gaze returned to her face.

"You're not bad looking yourself." Heather stretched one hand behind her back and unhooked her bra. "I've waited a long time for this."

"What?"

"You."

25

J AKE ALMOST STOPPED BREATHING. He froze, his hands on her hips and aching to move up her body, when he heard her words. She wanted him. Well, given where they were at the moment, that part wasn't too surprising. But that she'd been waiting for him?

He knew she didn't mean she was a virgin. There was no way she'd waited until they were nearly thirty for that. Besides, she said she'd been living with that Mitch asshole. Did he care that she'd been with others? No. It wasn't like he'd saved himself for her. What mattered was where they were now. Here in each other's arms.

"You're not the only one." He only hoped he could live up to her fantasies, because he assumed that if she'd been thinking of him that long, she had done as he had and thought about what it would be like.

Closing the distance between them, he covered her mouth in another searing kiss. His hand slid along her waist, and he marveled at how soft she felt, how had he gotten here again? Did it matter? What mattered was that he was here, and she was up for this, now he had to be sure he didn't screw it up.

He trailed his lips along her jaw and down her neck. She let her head fall back as he lavished attention on every inch he came across. One of her hands buried in his hair and seemed to urge him on. Pulling him close as small sighs and cries erupted from her mouth, urging him to continue.

When Jake reached her breasts, he teased one nipple with his tongue, flicking and circling the tip before sucking into his mouth, then releasing it to give the other the same attention. Judging from the way her fingers curled into his scalp and shoulder, along with the sounds she made, Heather approved. He loved the way they filled his hands, a perfect handful with only a little overflowing. He couldn't imagine her being more perfect.

Jake marveled at how responsive she was. He moved down her body from her tits, trailing kisses along her belly, loving that she was soft and pliant. He had been with scrawny girls and didn't like how they felt like they were all skin and bones and would snap in half if you were just a little too rough or bent them wrong.

When he reached the waistband of her jeans, he played a teasing pattern along the edge of the thick denim, looking up at her face to gauge her reaction. He wanted to take them off her, to strip her naked, but needed to make sure he wasn't moving faster than she was comfortable with.

Her head was thrown back against the mattress, her eyes closed as she seemed lost in the sensations. Before he had a chance to stop and ask if she was ready for more, her hands moved to her waistband and started shoving. He blinked in surprise when she didn't need to unbutton them before shimmying them off her hips, though he did love the way she moved and the way it made the soft parts of her jiggle. He leaned back and watched, taking in every breathtaking moment.

He loved that. Women were supposed to be soft and jiggle. Yeah, he liked to play with that jiggle, but he'd found most women didn't like it when you did. They seemed to be self-conscious about it, as if it wasn't supposed to be there. He hadn't yet figured out how to convince them they were wrong, but maybe he'd figure it out with Heather.

Once she'd kicked her jeans aside, he bent back over her, resuming where he'd left off. Jake continued to lick and tease his way down her body, but skirted around her core, teasing the sensitive skin at the crease where her thigh met her body. Tiny kisses and gentle nips with his teeth had her squirming and gasping. He smiled against her skin, enjoying her responses until she once more ran her hands through his hair, then fisted a handful and used it to steer his head where she needed it. Unable to resist the temptation any longer, he clamped his lips around the nub of her clit and paid it all the attention it had been denied.

"There, oh god, Aaron, yes!"

Her body bowed beneath him. He put one hand on her belly to hold her still so he wouldn't miss a single drop of the sweet nectar dripping from her center. As she started to relax, he doubled down, suckling her clit while sliding two fingers into her tight hot slit and curling them upwards to hit that hidden spot some men swore didn't exist.

Heather cried out again, almost coming off the bed as her body clenched and gushed. He lapped up every drop, enjoying the way her body went soft and pliant as she came down from the peak.

He moved up over her, watching her face. "Want more?"

"I want to return the favor, but I'm not sure I can. I'm not sure I could even stand right now."

"No worries. I know just what to do." He took the condoms he'd pocketed earlier when he'd been in the bunkhouse, just in case and tossed them on the bed beside her before stepping back and shedding his jeans, shoving them and his underwear off as quickly as he could, then went back to her.

He took advantage of her limp, almost boneless state and rolled her onto her side, leaving the leg on the bottom straight but bending the other at her hip so it looked like she was getting ready to climb a set of stairs, then moved over her so his knees rested on either side of her lower leg. Then, tearing one condom off the strip, he ripped the package open with his teeth and unrolled it down his length before leaning down to kiss her again, palming and kneading one tit as he reveled in her kiss.

"You ready?" he asked, still hovering just above her.

"Please." Her voice was low and husky, making his already rock hard dick throb. He bent, lining himself up with her opening, and pushed, then retreated, slowly working himself into her tight pussy, while trying not to lose his mind at how amazing she felt.

He needed her to come at least once more. He needed to feel her squeeze his cock as she exploded. He forced himself to concentrate on that, on making sure she got there before he could let himself go.

26

Heather had wondered what he was doing when he rolled her onto her side and moved her around like a rag doll, but he'd already made her feel so good, she wasn't going to argue. Hell, he could have folded her in half and stood her in the corner, her ass in the air, and she wouldn't complain if he wanted to make her body come alive like that again.

When he pushed inside her, despite the unfamiliar position, she found herself reaching for him, tugging him down and willing to do almost anything to get more. Her body seemed to have a mind of it's own.

With every stroke Aaron made, driving into her then retreating, the sensations seemed to multiply. Her scalp tingled, her toes curled and somewhere, someone screamed as her whole body clamped down and the world seemed to explode.

She saw stars, then seemed to float among them. Slowly, she became aware of the world and where she was again, and found Aaron had lain down behind her, curled against her with one arm wrapped around her middle.

"There you are." The low rumble of his voice vibrated through her whole body, sending waves of sensations she hadn't been prepared for spiraling through her.

"Hey." Her voice was rougher than she expected, and there was a slight ache in her throat.

"You okay?"

Heather blinked several times, trying to take stock of her body and making sure nothing was wrong, or at least more than it had been. Nope, everything seemed good. "I'm excellent." She wasn't ready to give up the amazing floating feeling he'd managed to give her.

"Good. Lay still and in a minute, I'll get up and clean us up."

"I'm in no hurry." She let her muscles melt as she relaxed into the warmth and security of his arms around her.

A knock on the trailer door made her groan. She didn't want to get up.

"Ignore them. They'll go away," Aaron said.

"You sure?"

"Yeah."

A moment later the knock came again, harder.

"They're not going away," she said, still not wanting to get up. She'd have to find something to wear, and even then, she was sure there would be no doubt what they'd been doing.

"Stay here," he said with a sigh. "I'll take care of it." His arm around her disappeared and she immediately wanted it back. Aaron pushed himself to his feet, then stepped out the bedroom door.

A moment later the pounding on the door resumed, and she wondered if Aaron had stopped along the way as someone shouted outside.

"I'm not going away until I see someone!" The voice was muffled but still audible.

She heard the door open, then the voice came again, clearer this time.

"Jesus. Put that thing away. Dude. Put some clothes on."

"You can see someone, what do you want?" Aaron didn't seem to care that he was naked.

"That sounded like something was wrong. Lurch said to make sure no one was being tortured or kidnapped."

That screaming she'd heard, had it been her? The scratch in her throat as she swallowed told her probably.

"We're fine. But you're not going to come in here and see her." Aaron's voice brooked no argument.

"Heather, you okay?" the voice came in a little clearer, as if whoever it was had shouted that last bit.

"I'm good!" she called back, fighting back a laugh at how ridiculous all this was.

"Okay then, I'll leave you be," the voice said in a normal tone. "And for Christ's sake, cover up before opening the door."

"Don't come pestering us if you don't want to see it all."

"Her I wouldn't mind seeing, but, dude. I did not need to see your dick. I think I'm scarred for life."

She heard the trailer door close and lay there still stifling her laughter at the whole situation when Aaron came back into the room. He'd stopped somewhere along the way because his condom was gone. He came up to the bed, gently rolled her to her back and used a wet washcloth to clean her up, then tossed the cloth aside before scooping her into his arms and shifting her over on the bed so he had more room to stretch out beside her.

"What was that all about?" she asked as he climbed onto the bed and lay down behind her.

"I didn't take you for a screamer, at least not like that, Lynnie." Aaron's voice was soft, gentle as he wrapped an arm around her and pulled her against him so her back rested against his chest.

Heather's face heated, but she wasn't about to admit that she didn't think she'd ever made quite that much noise before, at least not during sex.

"That's what he wanted?"

"Apparently someone thought either you could be being hurt or someone had managed to get onto the ranch and tried to take you. They sent Talon around to make sure neither had happened. They were looking out for you."

"Why did you open the door naked?" She frowned, she still couldn't figure that one out.

"To teach whoever was out there a lesson."

"What if it had been one of the women?" She didn't like the idea of him wandering around in front of any of them without his pants on for some reason. On top of that, she thought their men wouldn't like it either.

"They wouldn't have sent one of the women around to check on you. And a woman wouldn't have beat on the door like that. Besides, Talon had spoken before I opened the door, remember?"

She frowned and thought back, then remembered the muffled shout that they wouldn't go away until someone opened the door. "So, you knew it was one of them and chose to 'scar' him anyway?"

"Are you scarred?" The amusement in his voice was hard to miss.

"No, but I'm not one of your buddies either. Besides, I got to see you at your best."

He laughed, letting her know he thought the whole thing was as funny as she did. "He's not scarred, he's just an ass. It's not like he hadn't seen it before. Communal showers, remember?"

"Are you sure you want me imagining all of you in the shower together?" She bit the inside of her lip as she tried to keep from laughing at how she anticipated he would react.

"You better not be thinking about anyone but me in the shower." He almost hissed in her ear, his arm tightening around her middle.

She couldn't help herself. She loved teasing him. "Not even you and—" She held out, not saying the last one on purpose to get a reaction from him. She didn't have to wait long.

He growled in her ear, a low rumble that sent sparks spiraling through her previously stated body, and heat pooling low in her belly. "Watch it…" he warned.

"Me." She couldn't hold it back any longer and erupted into a fit of giggles, breaking loose from his hold and wiggling around to face him. "I wanted to see your face so bad on that one. But I couldn't help it."

"Thinking about you and me is acceptable. How big is the shower on this thing? Maybe we could try it out?"

"The shower's not too bad in here, though it would probably be a tight fit with the two of us. That's not what I'd be concerned about though."

"What would you be concerned about?" Aaron asked as he tilted his head forward until his forehead touched hers.

"Hot water. The tank on this is like two or three gallons top and you have to turn it on in advance. Did we light the pilot light on that when we set up?" Now that she thought about it, she knew they hadn't. She'd made sure the refrigerator was up and running, but she'd forgotten what Matt had said about the water heater. Had he said it had a pilot light or that it didn't? She couldn't recall. "It doesn't matter. I don't need hot water tonight. And if I do, I'll go inside."

To tell the truth, she hadn't paid much attention. Maybe she'd have to call him and ask. But not tonight. No, she didn't plan on moving more than she had to, at least for a while.

"Totally worth the wait," she murmured as her eyes drifted closed.

27

Jake's eyes snapped open, and he was instantly alert. He wasn't sure what had woken him, but something had changed. He stared up into the darkness, waiting. Would whatever had woken him happen again so he could figure it out or would he be left wondering?

He didn't have to think about where he was, both the comfort of the bed beneath him and the warm, soft body curled into his side had told him the instant he'd awoken that he was still in Heather's bed.

Beside him, she flinched and whimpered. Now he knew what had woken him. Something in her dream was disturbing her. He didn't know if she was re-living a memory or simply having a bad dream, either way he didn't like it. He hated anything disturbing her sleep this way.

Trying not to disturb her too much he rolled toward her, so his body curled around hers, hoping she'd take his presence in the comforting, protective way he intended it, then snuggled her close.

When she whimpered again, he loosened his hold around her middle, then smoothed her hair away from her face with a gentle hand before carefully stroking her cheek.

"It's okay, Lynnie," he murmured softly. He wasn't trying to wake her, but hoped the words would penetrate her subconscious and sooth her. "I'm here. I'll keep you safe."

He continued to pet her for a couple of minutes, until she stilled, then quieted. He lay there several minutes longer, wondering what she'd been dreaming of and how he could keep her safe before drifting back to sleep himself.

Jake shifted in the saddle, rolling his shoulders, and rocking his head from side to side to stretch his muscles and keep them from getting too stiff.

"How are you doing?" he asked Heather through the headset in their helmets.

"I'm good. This isn't too bad. Your bike is way more comfortable than Matt's."

He flexed his hands on the handlebars, not sure if the surge of anger was from her being on the back of another man's bike, or comparing the two bikes. Even if the other man was her cousin, or that his bike was coming out on top. Neither should make his gut churn the way it did, but he couldn't help it. He liked the feeling of having her on the back of his bike as much as he'd loved being in her bed last night. He didn't even mind the ribbing the guys had given him, both yesterday, and this morning before they'd hit the road. While he might never say it out loud, he knew he deserved it because of the things he'd said to them.

Now, with her against his back, he didn't care what they said to him, as long as they didn't say it to Heather or make her feel bad. He'd take all the shit they wanted to give him but at the same time, he'd do his damnedest to protect her from any of it. "We'll be stopping soon."

"Again? Already?"

They'd only been on the bike for about ten minutes, this time. But they'd spent three hours on it so far, plus the stops they'd made at Mt. Rushmore and the Crazy Horse Monument. They still had a good two hours home. But the next stop was for food.

"I heard your stomach rumbling as we wandered around the visitor's center at Crazy Horse. If the café hadn't been closed, I would have gotten you something to eat there."

"No, I'm glad you didn't. I'd rather have waited."

A few minutes later they pulled into town, at Jake's signal, Talon moved to the front of the group and led them to the main drag through town where he turned west. He'd already talked to the prospect about letting him find them parking, since he'd grown up not far from here and knew the town best. They hadn't gone far when they encountered a row of several empty parking spaces. Talon maneuvered his bike to block traffic, not that there was anyone coming at the moment, and signaled to Jake for people to park here.

Jake backed his bike into the space closest to where Talon sat astride his bike, leaving space for the prospect to get in, then killed the engine. Heather climbed off, then he dismounted, stepping over to where Talon watched and nodding to him once everyone had backed into line, then he kept an eye on traffic while Talon parked his own bike.

Once everyone had parked and dismounted, they stood clustered on the sidewalk, just milling about.

"All right. This main drag," Jake used one hand to motion the street they were on, but toward the east as they were close to the edge of town to the west, "is dotted with eateries, shops, and museums. I figured by the time we got this far, we'd be ready for a bite and to stretch our legs a bit. We'll gather back here at—" he glanced at his watch, then did a bit of math in his head, making sure to give everyone plenty of time to wait for food to be prepared, then to eat, "three o'clock. You know how it works, if something changes, you can't make the meet for whatever reason, reach out to me or Lurch. Go have fun. But not too much fun."

He watched as several couples drifted away, then turned to Heather.

"What are you in the mood for?"

"I don't know, I haven't thought about it. What is there?"

"Why don't we take a walk and look?" He motioned down the street with one hand.

"Sounds good to me."

They hadn't taken more than five steps before she slipped her hand into his. It felt a little odd at first. Unfamiliar. But she had reached out to him, and he wasn't going to tell her no. Not unless he absolutely had to, and at least this time, he didn't have to.

28

After eating in a small café, Heather enjoyed strolling down the street of the little town where they'd stopped for lunch. It was a pretty town, and she could tell, set up for tourism with a street full of trinket shops, cafes, and grills, all set up so you could park and hit them all without having to drive from one to another. It made for a great break from the road, whether on a bike or in a car.

"This is nice. How did you find it?" she asked, knowing he hadn't been on the ranch all that long.

"Talon mentioned it when I suggested we take the Arizona chapter to Rushmore."

"Is that why you had him lead us into town? Because it was his idea?"

"No, that was because he's familiar with the town. He grew up not far from here. It just made sense for him to get us parked rather than have me wander around hunting for a good space where we would all fit."

She nodded, watching the windows of the stores they passed.

"Seeing something you want?" Aaron asked when she stopped to peer in a window for a moment.

"Not really, just wanted a better look at something."

"We can go inside and look."

"No." She shook her head. "I'm good. But thank you." She didn't have a lot of cash left and she didn't want to spend it if she didn't need to. She had taken Matt's warning not to use her credit or debit card's to heart and hadn't touched them since that night in Tennessee when he'd had her get all the cash she could.

Heather didn't know if Mitch or any of those jerks he'd been mixed up with were still looking for her, but just in case, she wasn't going to make it any easier for them than she had to. If that meant not buying a few little trinkets she didn't need anyway, she could do it.

As they made their way back to where they'd parked the bikes, she watched Aaron's face and wondered what he was thinking. He'd been nothing but fun, nothing but great to be with and she wondered if he was always like this or was it a face he was putting on for her.

She had no doubts that he had a hard side, nearly everyone did. But was it something he only dipped into when he needed to, or was it something he worked hard to keep hidden?

"What you thinking, Lynnie?" he asked when he noticed her watching him.

His use of his twist on her middle name sent sparks of heat through her, though she couldn't have pinpointed why. Could it be because he was the only one who used the name? or just because it was him? Things between them had moved faster than she'd planned, not that she regretted it. He'd made her feel things the night before that she couldn't say she'd ever felt before.

"Just thinking about you," she said, still watching him as they walked hand in hand.

He shot her a frown, and she wasn't sure if it was because he didn't believe her or he didn't think he was worth her thoughts.

"You ready to get back on the bike?" He watched her as he asked.

"I am." She assumed he was looking for any sign she wasn't being truthful with him, but she didn't have to hide what she was feeling. She hadn't lied earlier when she'd said his bike was more comfortable than Matt's. She didn't know if that was on purpose or not, but it made her wonder how many other women Aaron had on the back of his bike. She hadn't wondered that about Matt's not because of how uncomfortable it was, but because she'd been on the bikes for different reasons. Matt, she expected to have had several women and didn't care. She was only there as a relative who needed help. But things were different with Aaron.

The more she thought about Aaron, his bike and who he might have had on it in the past, the more agitated she got so she did her best not to think about it.

"What's wrong?" he asked.

"Nothing." She shook her head. She didn't want to get into it now. Maybe not ever. He wasn't the kind to lie to her, and she wasn't sure she wanted to know if there had been others where she was now. Right now, it was too much. If there had been others, did that mean she would be just as short lived? Or if there hadn't been, did that mean something else? She wasn't sure which she wanted, or which she could handle at the moment, so better to put off the discussion she was sure was coming, but still wasn't ready for.

"Come on, Lynnie. If you can't talk to me, who can you talk to?"

She watched him for a moment then took a deep breath and let it out in a rush trying to push her worries out of her mind. "It's nothing, really. Just me over thinking things. Give me a bit with it. If I can't get past it on my own, I'll talk to you, okay?"

"I can live with that." He continued along the sidewalk beside her, swinging their joined hands between them. "How long?"

"How long what?" she asked with a frown.

"How long until you share it with me if you can't figure it out?"

She blinked, not sure she'd heard him right, then playing it over again. He wasn't asking just to make her feel better. He wanted to know what was on her mind. He cared. He cared enough to give her time and wanted to know when he could ask again.

"Can you give me until tomorrow?"

Aaron tugged her to a stop, turned to look at her before cupping her cheek with a free hand. She met his gaze and the world around them seemed to fade until the only things that mattered were the two of them.

"Lynnie, I'd wait until the end of time for you. Please try to be patient with me. I'm just a rough, crass biker, but if you let me, I'd set the world on fire to take care of you."

Heather had to lock her knees to keep from falling as they wanted to go weak. When had anyone ever said something so freaking perfect to her? Never. That's when.

Was she ready for this? Were her second thoughts, her doubts because she wasn't ready to let go and trust someone? That's what she'd have to figure out. Hopefully, before he asked again tomorrow. Because the last thing she wanted to do was lose the one person she'd been waiting on for most of her life.

29

Jake shifted in the saddle, standing in the stirrups to lift himself a little higher as he tried to look over the small ridge between the field where he was checking on the cattle and the road. A plume of dust told him someone was headed up the road and he wanted to know who it was. A red pickup truck that looked older than he was, though it was in excellent shape. It didn't look restored, just well cared for. Especially since Heather was back at the ranch house with out him.

She'd been asleep when he'd gotten up and had only woken briefly before he'd left. Jake smiled to himself as he remembered her sleepy voice when she'd rolled over and found him gone.

"Where'd you go?" she mumbled.

"I've got to go to work," he said as he pulled up his jeans.

"I'll get up and have coffee with you."

"No need."

"Then I'll make you breakfast." She fumbled with the blankets, trying to sit up.

"The prospects have breakfast all ready. Go back to sleep. Get up when you're ready. There will be food then too."

"You sure?" She blinked owlishly.

"I'm sure. Get some more rest. I'll be around later."

"Okay." She gave in and lay back down, pulling the blanket up to her chin. Unable to resist, he leaned over and kissed her forehead.

"Rest well, Lynnie," he whispered, then grabbed his boots and gone out into the living space of the trailer to put them on and retrieve his shirt before getting started on the day.

His phone buzzing in his pocket drew him back to the present. He pulled it out and saw Hex was calling.

"Yo, man, how you doing?" he said in way of a greeting.

"Something's happened. You got trouble." His old friend sounded worried, but not panicked, but from fifteen hundred miles away, why would he?

"What's up? What did you find?"

"The Wandering Sons have stepped up the search for your girl."

"Tell me what you know."

Tension built in Jake as he listened to Hex outline what he'd found out about the Sons' search for Heather. His horse, sensing his disquiet, pranced and sidestepped. Jake forced himself to relax, and turned the horse back toward the barn. Unease sat heavy in his stomach.

"What it all boils down to is, they're not out looking for her, but they want her."

"How bad?"

"Bad enough to put a reward for her return."

"A reward?" Jake couldn't believe what he was hearing. "How much and what are the conditions?"

"It's not good, man."

"Stop trying to ease me into it and just spit it out." The gnawing feeling in the pit of his stomach got worse.

"The reward is a hundred thousand. And the condition is no permanent injuries." Hex's voice told him that he hated having to relay the information. "I'm sorry to be the one to have to tell you. Is there anything we can do on this end?"

"Just keep an ear out. If anything changes, let me know. I've got to get back to the ranch and make sure she's still there."

He rang off and pocketed his phone, then urged the horse faster. The knowledge that someone had just arrived, and he didn't know who, was like a brick in his stomach.

Heather was in danger. And he didn't know where she was. Or who was in that strange pick-up.

Jake didn't know how long it took him to get back to the barn, but it was way too long. He rode into the barn yard, spotted Talon, and tossed him the reins even before he'd dismounted.

"Take care of him, I've got to check on Heather. Did you see who was in that truck?"

"What truck?" Talon asked with a frown.

Jake bit back the urge to snarl and yell. It wasn't the kid's fault. He didn't know what Jake had just found out, he couldn't understand Jake's desperation to make sure she was safe.

As soon as he was off the horse, he hurried toward the bunkhouse, and her trailer behind it. He'd cleared the barn where the motorcycles and other machinery were kept when he spotted the pickup parked near several other vehicles, empty.

He didn't see anything amiss, no one seemed disturbed by the new arrival, but they didn't know what he'd just found out. Jake scanned the area where people tended to gather in front of the bunk house, but he didn't see Heather there, so he angled himself toward the trailer. He needed to see her first, to make sure she was there and not hurt, then he'd find out who was in the truck and why they were there.

When he reached the trailer, he didn't bother knocking, but opened the door as he climbed the stairs, already calling for her.

"Heather!" He stepped inside, looked around and stopped. His shoulders sagged with relief. She sat on one end of the sofa, her legs folded beneath her as she sat sideways, facing someone. "There you are."

"I haven't gone anywhere, Aaron," she said with a frown, "Did you see who came to see me?" She motioned to the person on the other side of the couch. That's when Jake looked at them. He stared for a moment, as it took a moment for it to register, not because he didn't know him but because it was one of the last people Jake expected to see.

"Iceman." He stepped forward, holding out one hand. "It's good to see you man." This must be who had been in the red pickup. "That your classic pickup I saw out there?" He asked, just to be sure. The last thing he needed was to assume it was, be wrong, and have it belong to someone here to take Heather.

"It is."

"It's a nice truck. Restored?"

"No, just taken care of. It was my dad's, but it spent more time in the garage than on the road, as he had a commuter car he drove more often, still does in fact. It took me a long time to talk him out of that thing, but I'm glad I did. I love it."

"Looks like you're taking good care of it."

"What's up? I though you were out in the pasture?" Heather drew his attention back to her. He bent and kissed the top of her head.

"I was, but I got a call. It wasn't a good one, then I saw someone headed onto the ranch and I needed to make sure you were safe." He grabbed a chair from the dining table and set it close enough he could keep one hand on her, then sat. "What brings you down?" he asked to the other man.

Iceman lifted one brow, his eyes going back and forth between Jake and Heather in a pointed way, then he glanced toward the door before scowling at Jake, as if remembering that he'd come in without knocking first. Jake only met his gaze. He'd already been through this with the other man and wasn't going to rehash things. Especially not now.

"The Kings got a call," Iceman said, his gaze going back to Heather. "It seems the Sons, that's the club Mitch is mixed up with apparently, has put out a reward for your return."

Jake glanced at Heather to see how she was taking the news. Her eyes had gone wide, and she blinked several times but other than that, she seemed unphased. Jake knew that wasn't true, rather that she wasn't ready to let them see what she was feeling.

"A reward? To do what? Kill me?"

"No. Word is that if you're hurt, they won't pay."

Iceman's expression had gone soft, almost kind as he watched Heather struggle with the news. He hadn't given her the whole truth when it came to the reward and the conditions, but Jake didn't blame him for not telling her all of it. Who wanted to hear that she was wanted, and the only restriction was no permanent physical harm?

Hell, he didn't know if he could tell her that part.

"What was your call, the one that wasn't good?" She was watching him, waiting. He didn't know if she sensed it was the same news or if she was looking to distract herself while she processed the news.

"It was Hex, telling me the same thing." Jake tilted the top of his head toward Iceman, telling her that Hex had told him what her cousin had just told her.

"Huh, and with a truck you didn't know headed into the ranch. Is your horse all right?"

Jake didn't bother to try to stop the way one corner of his mouth quirked up. "Yeah. I rode him a little hard coming back, but I wasn't that far out, and I gave him to Talon to take care of as I arrived. By now he's probably brushed and in his stall with fresh feed and plenty of water. But I had to make sure you were okay."

"As if anyone here would let someone take me away." She reached over and picked up his hand, weaving her fingers with his before giving them a squeeze. "I don't think there's anywhere I would be safer."

"I would like to think so, but they let him in here." He tilted the top of his head toward Iceman again.

"But he's not someone who would hurt me," she said in his defense.

Jake turned to look at Iceman. "Did anyone even challenge you?"

"No. I got directions from Cowboy, and came down once I found out. I needed to see her and wanted to tell her about the reward face to face. But once I got here, I recognized the trailer and came straight here."

Jake scowled. "That's why I had to make sure you're safe. That should never have happened. Someone should have stopped him before he made it in here, if only to find out who he was or what he wanted." He'd have to talk to Lurch and let him know about it. He didn't like that Iceman hadn't been stopped and questioned. It left too many possibilities open for others to make it in and get to her. Perhaps hurt or take her.

It made him want to hurt someone. Preferably whoever was supposed to be watching the gate.

30

HEATHER DIDN'T KNOW HOW to feel. It was clear from the way Aaron had come in searching for her, that he was worried. And Matt wouldn't have driven all the way down if he didn't feel the same. But for some reason, despite their obvious concern and that she knew she should be worried, she felt safe.

It hadn't even occurred to her that Mitch or the idiots he was mixed up with would put out a reward for her, and she felt like it should have, but now that they had, she felt like at least they wouldn't be coming looking for her themselves. And they'd added the stipulation that she couldn't be hurt. So even if someone managed to take her, a long shot in her mind, they wouldn't hurt her or they wouldn't get paid.

"I'm fine. I told you I wouldn't go anywhere without letting you know," she said to Aaron. "And I meant it. I would eventually like to reach out to vets in the area, see if they're looking for a tech, but I'm not ready for that quite yet. Though I should do it sooner rather than later." She didn't mention that it was partly because she was running low on money. If she did, either or both would tell her not to worry about it, they had her covered. But she couldn't let them to do that. She needed to stand on her own two feet.

"It's a little more now, Lynnie. With this news, I don't want you off the ranch alone."

She started to protest, to say she was a big girl and could handle herself, but Jake placed a finger against her lips.

"Hear me out first, please."

She glared at him but nodded. He removed his finger and continued to talk.

"I'm not trying to keep you from doing what you want or going anywhere, I just want to make sure you're safe. I want to go with you if I can or send someone if I can't. With this reward, there will be plenty of less than ethical people looking for you, looking to make some fast cash. As much as I love your fire and spunk, please don't fight me on this."

The desperation in his voice, combined with the pleading in his eyes, stole all of the fight she'd been building toward. She didn't want to fight with him, especially when all he wanted was to take care of her. His words the day before echoed through her mind. 'If you let me, I'd set the world on fire to take care of you.'

Heather closed her eyes, took a deep breath, and said what might have been the hardest thing she'd ever said. "Okay. I won't go anywhere alone, at least for now."

While it wasn't the words themselves that were hard, letting go of her freedom, even temporarily, was. She only did it because she knew, deep in her heart, that as soon as it was safe, he would give it back. She trusted him to give it back. Because if he didn't, then she'd be forced to take it and if she had to do that, then she'd never trust him again. She could only hope she wasn't wrong in trusting him like she had been when she'd trusted Mitch.

"Thank you, Lynnie." Aaron's voice had gone soft. She kept her eyes closed, as he used one finger to lift her chin, then placed a gentle kiss on her forehead. "Are you sticking around?" The way his voice changed told her he wasn't talking to her, but to Matt.

"I may stay for a day or two, but I can't stay more than that. I have to get back to work. I'd say I can just stay in here, but from the way you came in, I'm not sure I want to. Even out here."

She opened her eyes to find Matt looking around the room as if he was wondering if any surface was safe anymore.

"You can have my bunk in the bunkhouse, if you want it, or we can find a spare tent and bedroll and you can camp in the pasture with the Souls who are up from Tucson."

"I'll think about it. I have a bedroll in the truck. I might just unroll it in the back if the weather stays nice."

"I'll talk to Lurch, get it cleared. I'm sure there won't be a problem, but you know how it goes."

Matt nodded. "I'd appreciate it. Let me know if you need anything, or if I can help out with making sure she's covered."

Beside her, Aaron stood. "I'll go do that, if you'll stay here with her."

"Be happy to."

"I don't need babysitting," Heather grumbled, scowling at them both.

"Don't think of it as babysitting, think of it as guarding. And thank you for dealing with it, for me." Aaron bent and gave her a brief kiss on the lips. "Hopefully, it won't be for long. Then you can go and do as you please."

She watched as he left, wanting to call him back, to have him sit here beside her and tell her it would be okay. Not that she would ever do that or ask that of him. No matter how much she might ache for it.

"Things seem to be going well, if moving a bit fast," Matt's words reminded her she wasn't alone.

"What makes you say that?" She frowned and tilted her head as she watched him. She hadn't done or said anything for Matt to think things had moved quickly between her and Aaron.

He propped his head up on one fist, arm propped on the back of the sofa where they both sat and watched her a moment, both brows raised.

"What?"

"Do you want me to go point by point or just say it was obvious?"

"Obvious how?"

"Point by point it is." He took a deep breath, then watched her a moment longer. "First was the way he came in here. He didn't knock but came in yelling your name and you didn't even flinch, didn't act like his just walking in wasn't something he did every day."

She blinked but didn't want to give any indication that it was something Aaron did. He wasn't usually yelling her name that way, but he'd quit knocking after the first night they'd spent together.

"Second, after he shook my hand, he went to you and kissed your head, like it's something he does every day. You didn't react, as if it's something you've come to expect. Third, the way he grabbed the chair and moved it where he wanted. He didn't hesitate, he didn't look around. He's spent a bit of time here and he's comfortable with you. Comfortable enough, he doesn't hesitate to touch you, even the smallest touch, and my being here didn't faze him. Which tells me you two touch a lot, and probably in front of everybody here." He used his free hand to make a wide motion, that that could easily include everyone on the ranch. "Fourth, he offered me his bunk. Where else would he bunk but here with you?"

"What's wrong with being comfortable with each other? It's not like we're screwing on the picnic table in front of everyone." She ignored the last part about where Aaron would be sleeping.

"Cuz, I never said there was anything wrong with it, only that it was obvious things have moved quickly with you. And if you wanted to screw on the picnic table in front of everyone, and you were both into it, I wouldn't judge you for that. As long as I don't have to see or hear about it." He let an exaggerated shudder run through his body.

Heather lifted her foot and shoved at him. "Knock it off. Why don't we go see what they've got for lunch?"

31

It took Jake a few minutes to track down Lurch, who was at the house he shared with Kerry, in the office. Kerry let him in and told Jake that Lurch was in his office, pointed him in the right direction then went back to whatever she was doing. Jake stood in the doorway, watching as the older man scowled at something on a laptop screen to one side of the desktop, then down at the page in front of him, going back and forth a couple of times. Jake knocked on the open door and waited.

"What do you need?" Lurch asked with out glancing his way.

"You got a couple of minutes?" Jake didn't know if it was his words or his tone, but Lurch stared at him for a second then motioned to one of the chairs across the desk from where he sat.

"Have a seat."

Jake turned and looked toward where Kerry had gone in the kitchen and wondered how much she knew about the club. Better to be safe than sorry. He closed the door then went to the chair Lurch had indicated and sat.

"What's going on?" He glanced toward the closed door then back to Jake.

"First, are you aware that one of the Kings of Destruction is on the ranch?"

"I am. I checked the camera when I got the alert he'd come through the gate. I saw Iceman and figured he was here to see your girl. Since he's her family, I decided there was no need to intervene."

Jake nodded and took a deep breath, held it a moment, then let it out, trying to push out his irritation that no one had challenged Iceman before he'd gotten to Lynnie with it. He hadn't made it on the ranch undetected. Hopefully, no one else would either.

"I got a call from Hex. We've got a problem." He'd already told the chapter president, and ranch foreman, about the problem Heather had left behind in Alabama when he'd gotten permission for her to come and stay. Now he just had to give him the latest information.

"Tell me." Lurch leaned back in his chair and folded his arms across his chest while he listened.

"I need to come clean about something first," Jake said.

Lurch scowled.

"It's not something that impacts any of us, or even the Souls directly, so I didn't see a need to share it before. But in trying to find out about what was going on with Heather, I already told you I called Hex. He's an old buddy from my time in the Army. LI need to fill you in on what I've found out."

Lurch nodded. Jake had told him this much already.

"In looking into the club Hex is part of, the Savage Warriors, I discovered they're not what they appear to be."

Jake shifted in his seat as Lurch didn't say anything but continued to watch him.

"I guess I never thought about it, because it surprised me to discover they're like we are."

Lurch's brows shot up, but he didn't say anything.

"Gizmo told me first, then I checked with my contact at my department, and they confirmed." Jake knew he didn't have to tell the president who he was under. They all knew they were with someone but rarely knew exactly which one. Usually the tech sergeant of the club had info on them all, that had been Gizmo, but that was in Tucson. It looked like he was becoming that person here. It wasn't a position he'd particularly wanted, but he seemed to be the best fit, so far. He'd have to have that discussion with Lurch at some point, but not now. This was more important now. "The Warriors are like the Souls. I didn't say anything before because the fewer people who know, the better. Maintaining cover, you know how it goes."

Lurch nodded, then waved one hand in a rolling motion, indicating for Jake to get on with it.

"Anyway, Hex called me this morning. The Sons have put out a reward for Heather."

"Reward?" Lurch leaned forward, placing both elbows on his desk.

"Reward, a hundred thousand dollars for her to be returned to them, with 'no permanent physical harm'." Those last four words made Jake sick to his stomach, but he knew Lurch needed to know. He didn't know if he could tell Lynnie what they meant, but Lurch wouldn't have to be told. He would get the implications.

"Fuck." Lurch let his head drop forward. "You're right. We have a problem. There is no way we can let them, or anyone looking to collect that reward, get their hands on her. She's sweet and from what I've seen, pretty tough and resilient, but I don't know if she could come back from that. Does she know?"

"Some of it. I told her about the reward, but not how much or the conditions."

Lurch tilted his head from side to side, as if considering something. "You might want to reconsider telling her; if she gets stubborn about maintaining her freedom. And I know from experience women can get touchy about their freedom, not that I blame them, because some men are always looking for ways to control them." He held up one hand before Jake could say anything. "I know that's not what you're doing and

I'm sure she will too, but sometimes, fighting any restriction is so instinctual, they don't stop to think about the why or anything else."

Jake nodded. "Right now, she's agreed not to leave the ranch alone. I don't want to tell her she can't be alone ever, because that would make us all crazy in no time, but I'd like to set things up, so people check on her regularly. The next couple of days should be easy though, since Iceman said he'd be around to help out. He'll spend most of his time with her."

"Does he know about the reward?"

"He does. That's why he's here. He wanted to make sure we knew, and needed to make sure she's safe." While he might have a few issues with the man, his need to make sure Lynnie was safe wasn't one of them, though his trying to run Jake off could have become one.

"He going to stay in the trailer with her?"

Jake pulled a face. "Probably not. Honestly? I don't think I want him to, even if she wants it. I offered him my bunk, if he wants it. Or we could find him an extra tent. He said he wasn't sure what he would do yet, said he may just bunk in the bed of his truck, as long as the weather's clear."

"Whatever. We'll figure it out. There's plenty of food and another set of eyes while we get things figured out wouldn't be amiss." He leaned back in his chair again, watching Jake for a few seconds. "Anything else?"

"I think that's it, at least for now. I'll keep you updated on anything I hear from Hex. Or anything else I find out about the Sons. We should look into some kind of surveillance or alarm on the gate to let us know when someone comes in. If only to give us a head's up."

"Sounds good. And I'll see what we can do about the gate." He turned his attention back to the computer screen. Jake left, heading back to see Lynnie and see what she and Iceman were up to.

He found them seated at one of the picnic tables, drinks in hand as they chatted. Jake had been a little frustrated when he'd found the trailer empty, but knowing she would likely be with Iceman, he hadn't worried. Much.

After going through the bunkhouse, to make sure they weren't inside, he spotted them when he'd stepped out the front. Relieved, he'd grabbed a drink from the cooler, checking in with the brothers working on lunch to make sure they didn't need any help, then went to join his girl.

When had he started thinking of her as his girl? He shook his head as he realized it had been before she'd even gotten to the ranch. He briefly wondered how she'd take it if he called her that out loud, then decided to find out.

He went to where they sat on opposite sides of a table, stepped over the bench, and settled in beside Lynnie. He threw his arm over her shoulders, leaned over, and kissed her cheek.

"What are we up to?" he asked as he sat.

"Not much. We were trying to decide what to do this afternoon." Lynnie dropped her head on his shoulder as she spoke.

Jake liked that she didn't change the way she acted or touched him in front of her cousin.

Lunch was called and they all got up to get plates before returning to their table and dug in. As they ate he contemplated what they could do. Then an idea struck him.

"How about we borrow some of the bikes from the ranch and go out riding?"

"Riding?" Lynnie asked, her nose crinkled as if she wasn't sure of the idea.

"Yeah, but not like the ride yesterday. These are dirt bikes, and you'll get your own bike or if you're not comfortable on your own on only two wheels we can get you a four-wheeler. It's fun, but a different kind of fun than the kind of ride you've been on recently."

"Oh! That kind of bike. I'd prefer a four-wheeler, but I'm in."

"Let me go let someone know what we're doing. I'll meet you in that barn," he pointed to the barn where they kept the bikes and equipment, "in about five minutes. If you brought your helmet, you might want to grab it, but we've got extras, if not," he said to Iceman before dropping a kiss on top of Lynnie's head, standing hand leaving the table.

32

Heather lifted her butt off the seat and hit the throttle, letting the four-wheeler bounce and roll over the uneven terrain without rattling her teeth. She twisted around to see how close the guys were behind her and found they were catching up. Swiveling back around, she considered going faster, but decided to do something different. Instead of pushing the throttle harder, she released it, then hit the brakes, letting the guys zip past her. As soon as they'd gone past, she cranked the handlebars all the way to the right and hit the throttle again.

As the ATV picked up speed, moving away, the guys swung wide, turning, to figure out where she was. Heather laughed and pushed the four-wheeler faster. When Aaron had first suggested bikes, she hadn't been impressed. She'd spent all day the day before on the back of his bike and while she'd enjoyed the trip, it wasn't something she wanted to do today or every day. But when she'd realized he meant dirt bikes and ATVs and that she'd get to drive her own, she'd been all in. Now, she was glad he'd suggested it. She hadn't laughed like this or had quite this much fun in... she couldn't say how long.

She didn't know how long they chased each other around the fields, going in circles, up and down the hillocks and doing stupid shit that did little more than waste time and gas, but she had such a good time, she couldn't care. Between that and how well Aaron and Matt had gotten along, she couldn't think of the last time she'd had a better day.

As they pulled the vehicles up to the gas tank to be filled before they were put away for the day, she remembered how she'd planned to spend the afternoon. Nothing like this, but she likely would have ended up just as happy and tired, though in a different way. Those plans had been thrown out the window as soon as Matt had shown up.

"Was it determined where you'll sleep?" she asked Matt after pulling off her helmet as the two of them took several steps away from the bikes and four wheeler, giving Aaron room to work. She hated the idea of putting him out of his own trailer.

"Jake said I can have his bunk in the bunkhouse. Since he won't be using it." Matt shot a scowl Aaron's way, as if he was unhappy knowing where he would be instead of in his bunk, but she thought it was as much for show as anything else.

"But will you use it?" Heather didn't know if she could sleep in a room full of men, or women, she didn't know. She wouldn't blame Matt if he couldn't either.

He lifted one shoulder and let it fall in a dismissive gesture.

Her gaze flickered to Aaron, where he was busy working the pump and filling each of the vehicles one by one several feet away.

"Matt?" She wasn't going to let him refuse to answer, even if it meant giving him the bed in the trailer while she took the couch. Aaron could sleep in his own bunk if Matt was going to be difficult.

He took a deep breath then forced it out his nose. "I'll make do. Either in the bunk or the bed of my truck. I kind of like the idea of sleeping under the stars. It's been too long since the last time I did it."

"You can have the bed." She watched his face, looking for any kind of tell, any reaction that would tell her what he was thinking. "I'll take the couch."

"The hell you will." Matt spoke between clenched teeth. "The last thing I'll do is take the good bed while putting you between me and the door. If that asshole," he tilted his head back toward where Aaron was hanging up the gas pump. "Wasn't already going to spend the night in your bed, then I'd be on the couch, between you and anything that might come through the door."

"No one will come in at night. No one knows where I am."

"And we'll do our best to keep it that way. But I'm not so sure no one knows where you are, and I'm going to do my damnedest to make sure nothing happens to you. That may be the only thing he and I have in common." Matt glared in Aaron's direction, then without saying anything, took off toward where Matt had kicked up one stand and was walking the bike the few feet to the barn to put it away.

Heather shook her head. There was no way to get someone like Matt to see that she could take care of herself. He thought she needed him to protect her, and she had to admit, she liked the idea of being protected, but she wouldn't let him keep her from doing what she felt was right. No matter what it was. With a sigh of her own, she went to the vehicles and stepped up onto the four-wheeler before starting it and driving it into the barn where it belonged.

"Well, what now?" she asked after Aaron took their helmets and hung them back on the wall where he'd taken them from earlier.

"Now, it's almost dinner time," Aaron said after consulting his watch. "After that we can join everyone around the firepits like last night, we can go into the bunkhouse and join in on the gaming tournaments, we can retreat to the trailer and do our own thing. Or we can skip dinner with the rest of the club, go into town and do our own thing. It's up to you guys."

"What's this about food?" Matt asked, rubbing his belly idly.

Heather laughed. Matt wasn't greedy but she'd never known him to turn down food, no matter how good or bad it might be. Not that the food on the ranch was bad. Despite that it seemed to be the prospects doing all the cooking, she'd found the few meals she'd had here so far to be nothing but good. Was it gourmet restaurant fare? No. But it tasted good and there was more than enough for everyone and that was more than she could say about her own cooking. Sure she could make enough for everyone, but whether they wanted to eat what she'd cooked was a different matter. She could barely boil water without trouble.

Okay, so she might be exaggerating, a bit. She could make a few, simple meals, but nothing like what these guys seemed to be doing and definitely not in the volume or frequency. Mostly she lived on sandwiches, scrambled eggs and fast food. Not that she had much option for fast food out here.

"I'm up for whatever you guys want to do. Dinner sounds good, as always. After that, firepit, games, trailer, I'm up for whatever." She wasn't much for video games, but she'd sit and watch while the guys played if that's what they wanted to do and be happy just to be able to spend time with them.

"Food it is. We'll figure later out when it gets here." Aaron motioned for them to leave the barn. Heather led the way, Matt not far behind her. Aaron brought up the rear, turning out the lights and closing the door behind himself.

"I don't know about you two, but I need to wash up a bit before I eat. If you don't mind, I'm going to step into the trailer for a few minutes."

"No problem. I'm going to do the same in the bunkhouse," Matt said.

Heather headed for the trailer, stepping up inside and heading for the bathroom. As she washed her face, she got a good look at herself and realized she needed more than just her face and hands washed. Her clothes probably had five pounds of dust and dirt on them.

Without thinking much about it she peeled out of her clothes and dropped them into the basket she'd put in the shower for dirty clothes. She would shower in the bunkhouse so she might as well get some use out of the space.

She pulled the band from the end of her braid and was working her fingers through the weaving on her way to the bedroom wearing nothing more than her bra and panties when the door to the trailer opened.

"Who's there?" she called out, freezing. She wanted to scream because she hadn't been able to keep her voice from shaking. Her heart thundered in her chest. The pistol Matt had insisted she bring with her was next to the bed. She hadn't thought she'd need it.

"It's me, Lynnie," Aaron's voice came back.

She leaned back against the door frame, letting her head fall back as she took a deep breath in relief. There were people everywhere. No one was here on the ranch to kidnap her, and she should have known better.

"Are you all right?" The concern in his voice made her open her eyes and turn to look at him, her head still propped against the door.

"Yeah, I just wasn't expecting anyone, and when you came in, every stupid possibility flashed through my head." She rolled her eyes at her stupidity, stood, and continued into the bedroom. "It wasn't pretty. Especially after this morning's news."

"I'm sorry. I didn't want to scare you. Either this morning or just now. I didn't know you were changing, or I would have given you a head's up that I was coming in." He glanced down at himself. "I realized how dusty I am and was going to grab a clean shirt." One corner of his mouth quirked up as his gaze skimmed down her body then back up. "I should have known you'd think of the same thing."

She closed the distance between them, wanting to feel something good, something to replace the cold flash of panic that lingered in her veins. Without asking, she slid her hands up under the hem of his shirt and shoved it up, sliding her hands along his torso as she did. She wanted a kiss but wanted his dusty shirt out of the way first.

Aaron took the hint, reached behind his head, and tugged the shirt off. He tossed it into the corner he'd been using for his dirty clothes. Heather stepped into his personal space, slid her hands around his waist and stretched up to press her lips against his. His hands came around her body, smoothed down her torso and came to rest for a moment on top of her butt.

She relaxed into him letting his warmth and strength surround her for a moment. Aaron deepened the kiss, his hands smoothing down over her ass, then grabbing and lifting. She wrapped her legs around his waist and lost herself in his touch. How did he seem to know just what she needed?

33

It took everything in Jake to break the kiss, but he couldn't put her down, not yet.

"Lynnie, you make me lose my head." He placed a soft kiss on the side of her neck then lowered her back to her feet. "Put some clothes on or we'll miss dinner."

"I could go for that."

"I wouldn't complain, but if we did it, then your cousin would come looking for us. Is that what you want?" If it was, he'd deal with it. Anything to put a smile back on her face. He hadn't intended to, but when he'd found her leaning against the wall, trying to catch her breath, he realized he'd scared her.

Jake wanted to kick himself. He should have known better than to just come in like that, without at least calling out as he stepped inside to let her know it was him. He didn't know if Iceman would do the same, but he'd stop and talk to him later just to be sure neither of them scared her like that again.

She stared up at him for a moment then shook her head. "We better not. He'll be gone soon enough, then we'll have more time."

Jake wasn't sure about that. Yeah, they might have a little more once her cousin went home, but then they still had both chapters here, at least for a few more days. And once Tuck and the rest of the Tucson chapter left, it was back to the everyday work of the ranch. She might find she had a lot more time on her own than she really wanted.

Hopefully, they'd be able to put an end to this bullshit with the Wandering Sons and that fucking reward, then as much as he hated to think about it, she could go back to her life. He just wanted enough time to convince her that she could have that life here, with him. She didn't need to go back to Alabama to go on with her life. But hadn't she said something about finding work here? Did that mean maybe he could convince her to stick around?

He let her slide down his body, making sure she stayed steady while she got her feet under her, then he leaned down and kissed her lips before standing again.

"Let me grab a shirt." He glanced down her body, hating to have to let her go. "And you might want to find something to put on too. Then we'll go eat. Before you know it, it will be bedtime and we'll be right back here again." He kissed the tip of her nose before releasing her and going to find himself a shirt.

Would he rather have taken her to bed, to hell with dinner? Of course, but if his coming in scared her like that, he wanted to talk to her cousin before he did the same and scared her again.

"I need to go check on a couple of things with the prospects and Lurch. I'll meet you outside in a few." Jake tugged his shirt over his head and on, then turned for the door. He wasn't lying, he would check in, but his main goal was her cousin and preventing a repeat of the panic she'd gone through when he'd come in.

"Sure. I'll be out in just a few."

"Take all the time you need. It's not like we'll run out of food or there's a schedule we need to stick to."

Jake made his way out, through the bunkhouse, looking around for Iceman on his way, then stopped by the outdoor kitchen where the prospects from both chapters worked under London's supervision. After making sure nothing there needed his attention, he scanned the clearing they were using as a gathering spot. There Iceman was, just coming around the building. Jake didn't know where he'd been, but if he had to guess, he'd say the other man's truck, which he'd parked next to Lynnie's next to the trailer.

"Hey, just the man I was looking for," he said as stepped up to Iceman.

"I'd think you had your fill of me today," Iceman said with a grin that faded when he saw Jake wasn't laughing.

"Let's sit down for a sec." Jake motioned to an empty picnic table.

"Is something wrong?"

"Not really but I wanted to give you a head's up. I just went out to the trailer to change shirts, didn't want to knock dirt off the one I was wearing into my dinner. I didn't think much of it, I opened the door and went inside, like she told me to when she first got here."

"Okay?" Iceman made the one word a question, because he didn't see a problem with what he was being told apparently. That made Jake feel a bit better. He wasn't the only one who hadn't thought about it.

"I hadn't made it back to the bedroom yet when she called out asking who was there. I could tell from her voice that she was scared. I realized how scared when I saw her. She was all but trembling, even knowing it was me by then."

"And you wanted to tell me because?"

"Because I wanted to warn you not to just go inside. I don't know if you would, but it's your place, I wouldn't blame you if you did, but call out, let her know it's you, something."

Iceman was quiet for a moment, watching Jake with narrowed eyes that made Jake wish he knew the man better, that he had some inkling what he was thinking.

"You think it was the news about the Sons and the reward?" Iceman asked after a moment.

"I do." Jake shrugged. "I'm not saying you shouldn't have told her. I was coming to do the same thing. She needs to know what she's up against. I just want you prepared, so you don't scare her like I did."

"I'm sure the talk we had while you were gassing up didn't help."

"What was that?" Jake had noticed they'd moved out of the way while he'd been busy, but he hadn't paid any attention to what they'd been talking about.

"She told me that if I didn't take your bunk, she would give me the big bed in the trailer while she took the couch. I told her why that wouldn't be happening. The last thing I would do is put her between me and the door. I told her that. I told her I will probably sleep in the bed of my truck, partly because I like the open sky, partly because that will put me as a first line of defense if anyone approaches her trailer."

"Well, second or third. We've got alarms on the front gate that let us know when someone comes through, but I get what you're saying. And I appreciate it, but you're right that conversation then my not letting her know who it was when I went inside, didn't help."

"No, it probably didn't. I'll be careful. I don't want to scare her more than necessary, but I won't hold things back from her either." Iceman pinned him with a warning look. "I wouldn't suggest you do either. If she finds out you've held something back from her, even if it's to protect her, she'll tear you a new one, and it may not be possible to regain her trust. She doesn't trust most people easily. That she trusts you is the only reason I didn't stop her from coming down here. Well, that and Cowboy said the Souls can be trusted. If I had any thought that you wouldn't protect her as hard as I would, she wouldn't be here, even if I had to install a room in my basement to lock her in."

"That went dark quickly," Jake said, trying to keep things from getting too dark. Heather came out of the bunkhouse, having obviously cut through like he had. Jake nodded in her direction. "I know better than to keep things from her. But I'll do what I have to in order to keep her safe. She's important to me." The last thing he was prepared to do was to tell her cousin how he felt about her before he said it to Lynnie. But first he had to figure it out himself.

"I'm going to go wash up, I'll be back in a minute." Iceman pushed himself to his feet and headed for the bunkhouse. Jake watched as he stopped to talk to her for a few seconds, then continued past her and inside.

34

Heather rolled her eyes at Matt's grouchy overprotective tendencies and turned to find Aaron watching her. She smiled and put a little strut in her walk as the distance to where he sat.

"Are you waiting for me before you eat?" She gave the empty table in front of him a pointed look.

"Yes and no," he said, he tilted the top of his head toward the outdoor kitchen. "Food's not done yet. But I would have waited for you even if it was." He reached across the table and grabbed her hand, tugging her around the table until she stood beside him. "Have a seat. I'll get us something to drink then we can talk about what we want to do tonight."

She stepped over the bench and sank down beside him. He twisted around to plant a sweet, gentle kiss on her lips.

"What do you want to drink?"

"Whatever."

"Water, soda, beer?"

"How about a beer and a water?"

"Coming right up." Twisted around, throwing first one leg, then the other over the seat before he headed for the kitchen area and the ice chests that sat under a couple of tables.

She looked around, taking in the people lounging around the unlit firepit, sitting at other tables, and moving around the kitchen area with purpose and wondered how many of them knew about her problem. Well, all of them knew at least the basics. They had to in order to be on the lookout in case someone came on the ranch looking for her, but how many knew about the news that had come in this morning. The reward.

Neither Matt nor Aaron had mentioned how much the reward was but how many here needed money? How many would cash in on that offer by telling the people after her where she was?

Ideally, none, but she hadn't made it to nearly thirty years old, still believing in best case situations. She'd long ago learned that individual people were generally good, some even wonderful, but as a collective, people sucked and would generally let you down.

Her best hope was that these people had enough invested in Aaron not to do that to her.

That reminded her of the Kings, and all the people in North Dakota she'd met or spent time around. How many of them knew and could be trusted? Thankfully, the only person who knew where she was up there was now here with her. She had no doubts about Matt. Not just because he was family. She had some members of her family who would turn her over for a few hundred dollars in reward. Not that either Matt or Aaron had mentioned how much the reward was. For all she knew, that's all it was. A few hundred dollars and not enough to tempt the people around her into betraying her secret. At least that was her hope.

"You're thinking too hard," Matt said as he stepped over the bench and sat across the table from her. "We need to do something about that."

Heather scrubbed one hand down her face, trying to wipe away the thoughts that someone would turn her in for the reward money, then looked up and met Matt's gaze.

"How do you suggest we do that?"

"I don't know. Maybe after dinner we see if we can find some cards. I'm sure we can distract you for a while. Maybe a few hands of poker, maybe something else. What would you like to play?"

She tilted her head and watched him for a moment, thinking back to what kind of games they'd played when she'd been growing up.

"I wonder if anyone has a deck of Phase 10 cards?"

"What was that?" Aaron asked, setting her drinks in front of her, before setting his own where he'd been sitting before and handing another to Matt.

"I was just wondering if we can find a deck of Phase 10 cards around here." She twisted the top off the water bottle he'd brought her and took a long pull.

Aaron paused in mid-drink, turned, and looked at her a moment, then lowered his drink. "Phase 10? I think I can find a deck. Maybe a couple if you're open to others joining us."

"Sure. The more the merrier." She remembered the fun of a big group playing when they'd been teenagers, could it be any less now that they could drink while they played?

"I'll find us the cards after we eat. Dinner's almost ready." He tilted his head toward the kitchen area.

She glanced over to see what looked like the prospects setting things up on the buffet line. As if the sight reminded her stomach how long it had been since she'd last eaten, her stomach rumbled. Heather shook her head and wondered why the sight of food being ready would do that, it wasn't like her stomach had eyes.

"LINE UP!" London's shout from the head of the line stopped her from saying anything. Leaving their drinks at their seats, the three of them, along with many of the others scattered around the area, stood, and made their way to the kitchen. Heather was fifth in line, and as she stepped up to the table and picked up a plated, she realized that the guys had disappeared. Looking around she noticed that there were only women in line with her. Not wanting to hold things up, she moved through the line, helping herself to whatever she wanted, as she'd already learned that was how meal times worked on the ranch.

When she'd made her way through the line, she stepped out of the way and took a look at the entirety of the line. Sure enough, like the run she'd gone on with Matt, the one where she'd run into Aaron again, the women were first, and the men followed them through the line. This wasn't how they'd been doing things when she'd first arrived, and she couldn't help but wonder what had caused the change. Not that it really mattered. As far as she'd seen, there was plenty of food for everyone, so it didn't matter if you were first through or last through, you'd get enough to eat. And if things worked the same way as yesterday, there would be stragglers. Couples that were farther away, or busy, when the dinner call went out. And there would be plenty for them as well.

Heather took her plate to the table where she'd left her drinks and sat, digging in, and eating while her food was hot. As she ate, she was joined by Elyse and Kerry.

"Mind if we join you?"

"Not at all." She motioned to the empty space at the table. "How has your day gone?" she asked other women as they sat and got comfortable.

"Good," Kerry said.

"Quiet," Elyse put in. "What have you been up to? Your friend came to see you right?"

"Matt's my cousin, but yeah." She debated whether or not to mention the reward to them, but decided not to. If they needed to know, their men would tell them.

She decided then and there that there was only so much she could do about it. She could be alert and not let anyone sneak up on her, but most of the rest was out of her hands. And while she could waste a lot of stress and energy worrying about what would happen, what could happen, that's what it was, a waste. She might as well let Aaron and his friends do what they said they would. She trusted him, so she would trust his judgement.

And Matt would be here another day or so. Between the two of them, and the rest of the men on the ranch, she would be safe.

"We're going to see if we can find some cards to play after dinner. You're welcome to join us if you like."

"Oh. I can't remember the last time I played cards with someone other than Mac," Elyse said.

"Mac plays cards?" Kerry tilted her head as she looked at Elyse.

Heather's gaze flicked to the large, bearded man currently fixing himself a plate. She could see why Kerry would be surprised, but why not? All kinds of people played cards or other games, all the time. What they looked like had no impact on the things they enjoyed. How many people had told her she didn't look like a vet tech?

Elyse nodded to Kerry but turned to look at Heather. "What are you looking at playing? Anything specific? I've got some cards with us."

"My preference is Phase 10, but if we can't find enough decks for everyone to play, there are options." Heather tilted her head back to lookup at Aaron as he joined her at the table, setting his plate down and kissing her forehead as he sat.

"You finding people to play with us later?" he asked.

"I am."

"Good."

One by one, the rest of their men joined them, including Matt, and they fell mostly quiet as they ate.

35

"Did you have a good time this evening?" Jake asked as he peeled his shirt off and tossed it on top of the rest of his dirty clothes. Tomorrow he would gather all his dirty things up and wash them.

"I did." Lynnie yawned as she shimmied out of her jeans.

Jake found himself standing and watching her undress, his hand on the button of his jeans where he'd started to take them off, then got distracted by watching her ass wiggle in the tiny scrap of satin that barely covered anything.

"I haven't played cards like that in ages. We should do that more often." Her back was still to him as she took off her own shirt and tossed it aside before reaching back to unhook her bra.

Jake unbuttoned his jeans, glad for the extra room as he shoved them off his hips then down, his eyes never leaving Lynnie. She wasn't trying to give him a show. And that's what made it even sexier.

"Do you think the others will be up for it?" she asked, turning around to look at him. She froze when she spotted him watching her. "You don't care about cards or anyone else right now, do you?"

He bit the inside of his lips as he kicked his jeans aside and slowly shook his head and tried to keep from saying something that would get him in trouble, his gaze never leaving hers.

"Do I need to guess what you are thinking about?" She slid her hands slowly up her sides until she cupped her breasts.

Jake couldn't help but drop his gaze to watch as it felt like she was offering them up to him. His cock stiffened and he shook his head, watching the entire time as her index fingers circled and teased her nipples, wishing those were his hands. He ran the tip of his tongue over his lips, wishing it was her skin he was tasting.

He took a step toward her but stopped as she stepped backward.

Jake lifted his gaze to hers. He wasn't expecting what he found there. The amusement tinged with a bit of challenge.

"Is that how you want to play it tonight? Tease me? Are you going to give me a show?"

Lynnie's face turned pink. "Show?"

"You started this. Hop up there and show me how you like it." He motioned to the bed beside where she stood.

"What do you mean?"

"I mean you're going to show men how you play with yourself."

"I—I don't know if I can do that, not with someone watching." Her stammer only made him harder.

"It's not just someone, it's me, and you started it. I suggest you get started because I'm not touching you until you come at least once." He palmed his hard length through the cotton of his briefs, squeezed and ran his hand over his length before releasing himself. He lifted one brow in challenge.

He watched as she pushed the scrap of satin that was her panties off her hips then kicked them into the pile with the rest of her clothes before moving to the bed. Her expression and the bright pink shade of her face told him she was embarrassed, but he wanted to see how far she would take it. Would she do what he'd told her to?

He was tempted to go grab one of the chairs from the dining room table, so he could sit and watch while too far away to reach her so he wouldn't be tempted to move in before she'd met the requirement he'd given her. But he was afraid that if he walked out of the room, it would kill the mood, and he'd never get her started again. Instead, he moved around the foot of the bed and leaned up against the dresser there, crossing his legs at the ankles and folding his arms across his chest.

Lynnie wiggled and scooted across the bed until she was in the middle, but leaning against the wall at the head of the bed, knees and ankles together and folded in front of her. She smoothed one hand up her leg, pausing to make circles on her knee before continuing up her thigh. "Are you really going to make me do this?"

"Do you want to come tonight?" he asked, watching her face until she looked up and met his gaze.

"Yes."

"Do this for me. I'll make it worth your while." Jake did his best to let her see how hot he thought she was, how badly he wanted this. As if his dick wasn't hard enough to hammer nails and while not fully on display, it was plainly visible as he stood there in his underwear.

She started to say something, then stopped, bit her lip, and dropped her gaze.

"Say it."

"It might be a little easier if I wasn't the only one naked." She glanced up at him, her face turned even redder, then she dropped her gaze back to the bed in front of her.

"That's easily solved." He unfolded his arms, shoved his briefs off and kicked them onto the pile of his dirty clothes, ignoring the way his cock bobbed as he folded his arms and turned his attention back to her. "Better?"

"Actually, yes."

"Good. Now show me what you like. The sooner you quit delaying and get to it, the sooner you'll find out what your reward is."

"I'm sorry. It's not easy." She looked down at the bed again.

Jake couldn't take it any longer, he moved around and sat on the side of the bed, placed one finger under her jaw and used gentle pressure to get her to look up at him. When her gaze met his, he leaned in and placed a soft, sweet kiss on her lips.

"Lynnie. I've already seen and touched all of you. Hell, I've had my mouth on every inch of you. I just want to see how you make yourself happy. I want to see what you do, how to get you where we both want you to go."

"Will you do the same for me?"

"You want to watch me jerk off?"

"Seems fair if you want me to masturbate for you." She looked up at him through her lashes, as if the coy look would get him to agree. She needn't have gone to the trouble. He'd do it for her, and think it was hot while he did.

"Sure. But not tonight. Tonight, I want to see you, then show you what it does to me." He took one of her hands in his, wrapped it around his cock and squeezed so it was her soft hand on his skin, gripping him just the way he liked. "Maybe I'll show you in the morning, then let you practice making me feel good."

She smiled. "That sounds like a plan."

She leaned over as if to take his dick in her mouth, but he pulled both hands away and stood, moving out of her reach, out of the temptation of letting her run her tongue up and down his length.

He clenched his teeth and told himself he was focusing on her tonight, as he made his way back to the foot of the bed where he couldn't touch her, and she couldn't touch him. He folded his arms to keep his hands busy and away from his dick, then pinned her with his gaze.

Heather moved her hands to her breasts, letting her fingers play over her nipples, rolling them then pinching them tips before kneading and squeezing the entirety of a breast in each hand. Her eyes drifted close and her head fell back as she lost herself to the sensations.

Then her hands moved down her torso, skimming along the skin of her belly then down to her legs, she ran both hands along the tops of her thighs before moving them to skim up the sensitive skin along the inside. A soft whimper escaped her throat as one hand disappeared between her legs.

Jake cleared his throat.

Heather's eyes flew open, and she lifted her head to meet his gaze. "What?" Her voice had gone thick and husky.

"I can't see what you're doing." He let his gaze flick to where she still sat with her knees to one side, blocking his view.

"Oh, I guess that would help."

"A little, but I won't stop you if you need to close your eyes and pretend I'm not here, watching."

She didn't say anything, but her eyes drifted closed again. A few seconds passed then she shifted, she started with her knees and feet together in front of her, heels pressed against her ass and her hands back on her tits. Her fingers played with her nipples again, seemingly starting over. Not that Jake minded. Though he did wish it was his hands, his tongue and mouth teasing those pretty, tight nipples.

Slowly, her hands drifted down her body again, this time instead of keeping her knees together as her hands slid below her belly button, she parted them. Dropping her legs open so they lay splayed wide on the bedspread, her heels still pressed together, giving him an unobstructed view of everything she was doing with her fingers. They dipped into the cleft between her legs, circling and teasing the sensitive nub that hid there.

Jake forced himself to stay where he was, despite the urge to move in, to take over and to push her over the edge himself. No, he wanted to see her do it. Then he could move in, make her come again, and again if he wanted.

He didn't think he could get any harder, he wanted to move in and take over, to touch her so badly. But when her other hand dipped below the first, sinking first one finger, then two into her hot core, he almost lost his resolve.

One finger worked her clit, moving in circles around it then back and forth flicking the tip while her other hand worked in and out of her pussy. The soft gasps and change in Lynnie's breathing told him she was getting close. He fisted his hands where they sat in his folded arms and forced himself to stay where he was.

Her breath caught, her body tensed, her hands stopped moving as her back bowed. He didn't need to feel her clenching around him to know what was happening. A fine sheen of sweat covered her body as he dropped his arms, unclenched his fists, and crawled up the foot of the bed toward her.

"Here, love." Jake tugged the fingers from her leaking cunt, taking the time to suck them clean before setting her hand aside, then he moved her other hand as he moved in closer, dropping a gentle kiss against the top of her mound. He knew she was likely sensitive and didn't want to overstimulate her, but at the same time, he couldn't wait to get a taste. When her breathing returned to normal, he was careful how much pressure he used as he lowered his mouth to her core, licking and tasting every bit of her heat and moisture.

Taking advantage of the lubrication already there, he pressed two fingers inside, curling them to hit the sensitive spot toward the front of her entrance while he flicked his tongue back and forth over her clit.

Heather's hands found their way to his hair, tugging and pulling, trying to move him up, away from her core. He ignored her, determined to feel her clench around his fingers, to taste her pleasure at least once before he found his own.

"Aaron, please." Her words were husky with need.

"What, baby?"

"I need you. Inside me."

"Soon. Give me one more first."

Jake didn't know if it was his demand or the vibrations of his talking against her, but as if on command, her pussy clenched around his fingers, squeezing them tight as a wave of her slickness cascaded from her, filling his mouth. He savored the sweet, tangy taste of her pleasure.

36

Heather's body felt like a bowstring drawn tight. Colors burst behind her eyes and pleasure washed through her. She was barely aware of Aaron's hands sliding up her body, until something flicked across her nipples, sending renewed sparks of heat through her.

The thick, blunt head of his cock nestled against her opening was impossible to miss. It was just what she wanted, no, needed. She slid her hands down his body until she found the round globes of his butt, then squeezed and pulled. She needed him inside, she needed him to fill the empty, hollow feeling in her core.

"I just wanted to make sure you were ready."

The low rumble of Aaron's voice sent shivers through her as he thrust inside, sinking all the way inside her in one swift, hard thrust.

"OH!" She couldn't help but cry out as he filled her, sending more waves of pleasure crashing through her body. "More." She needed more. She needed him. Now.

Her fingers curled into him, pulling him closer, needing more, anything. She couldn't put it into words but as he withdrew and thrust back into her, her body clenched and seized, a haze of need and pleasure filled her mind, pushing out all thought but him. A wordless cry erupted from her throat, then, remembering the way they'd been interrupted the first night, she pressed her face into his shoulder, hoping to muffle the worst of her cries. Maybe keep people from coming to check on them. As wave after wave of pleasure washed through her, she lost track of what she was doing, lost track of what she was supposed to be doing and surrendered to the sensations and the peace it brought with it.

She didn't know how long it took for the world to become real again, but when it did, she realized Aaron lay on the bed beside her, his arms tight around her as if even as he tried to catch his breath and recover, he couldn't stand letting go. She liked that. She liked his holding her close, as if she was precious to him. She knew she should get up and clean up but before she had the energy to move, she drifted off to sleep, feeling safer than she had since Matt had shown up and surprised her.

LIGHT IN HER FACE woke Heather, reminding her that she'd forgotten to close the blinds after waking the same way yesterday. She rolled over and found the bed beside her empty. Running her hand over the space where Aaron had been the last time she'd gotten up in the middle of the night to use the restroom, she found the sheets cold. He'd been gone for a while.

She stretched, then lay staring at the ceiling for several seconds wondering what today would bring, before her bladder insisted that she get up and get moving.

After a visit to the bathroom, she stood for a moment, staring at the bed and debating whether or not to climb back in. She felt safe there. Like nothing would come looking to hurt her. It was silly, she knew, but she couldn't help the way it made her feel.

It only took a moment's internal debate before she discarded the idea. Instead, she picked up her clothes from where she'd tossed them the night before and put them in the basket in the shower. Oh... shower. She needed one. A quick check of the time told her the bunkhouse showers were reserved for women right now, so she pulled on some sweats, grabbed her shower bag and some clean clothes, stepped into a pair of flip flops, and headed into the bunkhouse and the showers there.

After her shower, freshly dressed and with wet hair, she carried things back out to the trailer, where she found Matt standing inside. He looked up as she opened the door and pinned her with a confused look.

"How did you get past me? When?"

"I don't know," she said as she stepped past him and toward the bedroom where she could put things away. "I didn't know you were even watching for me, so I wasn't trying to get past you. All I did was go inside to shower."

"You can shower in here."

"I know but there's more room in the bunkhouse. It's easier to shower in there."

He stared at her for a moment, then shrugged as if to say it was her business. "What's the plan for today?"

"I don't have one." She continued into the bedroom tossing her sweats across the edge of the dresser to wear again later, then put away her shower bag and straightened up the bed. "My immediate plans are to finish getting dressed, then go get some coffee, maybe a little food, and see what is planned for today. Don't you have work tomorrow? What time do you need to leave to make it home in time to get some sleep?"

"You let me worry about that."

Heather rolled her eyes. She hated it when he didn't answer a question with a real answer. She asked because she wanted to know how much time they had together. How long until there was one less person watching out for that club hunting for her.

"Whatever." She wasn't going to argue with him and the last thing she'd do was let him know she was worried. If she did, he might drag her back to North Dakota with him, or at least try.

She wouldn't make it easy if he did. She'd spent enough time lounging on his couch feeling sorry for herself.

She might not be exactly productive here, but she did have her own space, even if it was borrowed, and she felt a little more in control of her life. Hopefully, she could find a job soon. That reminded her, she should ask some of the women who lived here about local vets. She wondered if the ranch had someone they used when they needed someone to check out one of the livestock. That should be her first call.

She pulled a pair of socks out of the drawer, used her hip to close it as she decided to wear her boots, and tried to remember where she'd left them. After checking the closet, and finding them inside, she carried them into the front room where she found Matt still standing. He had his hands on his hips as he watched her as if he was expecting something.

"What?" she asked as she sat on one end of the sofa and began pulling on her socks.

"You didn't tell me what you're doing today."

"I told you what I have planned, which isn't much. On the other hand, I asked when you need to leave so maybe I could make plans with you, and I got blown off. I'm not real thrilled with that." She'd been going to let his answer go but when he called her on not giving the answer he'd wanted, she could do the same.

There were some things that might get the better of her, like knowing someone was offering money for her return. And others that she would never let just roll. And people thinking they knew what was better for her than she did, well, that was one of the things she just would not put up with.

When she'd stepped into both boots, she cast him one last glance that left no doubt how unhappy with him she was, then left. She wasn't about to wait around for him to figure out what he'd done wrong. She wanted coffee and food and now that she was dressed, she was going to go get both.

She'd filled a plate and was in the process of filling her travel cup with coffee when Matt stepped out the bunkhouse door and looked around. She was still half pissed at him and his attitude, so she didn't bother waving. Instead, she ignored him as she doctored her coffee, then carried it and her food to one of the tables and sat.

She was halfway through the food she'd gotten, and the caffeine was starting to hit her blood when Matt set a plate on the table across from her. He sat, stared at her for a couple of seconds, then spoke. "I'm sorry."

Her mood was a little improved from when she'd left him in the trailer, but not enough to let him off the hook for his bullshit. She stared at him in return, waiting for him to say more.

"I'm sorry I jumped all over you. I went in to check on you and you were gone. I was scared and took it out on you, I'm sorry."

"Thank you, and I didn't pass you. I stepped out of the trailer, took what is it? Six steps to the bunkhouse and went inside. I won't apologize for taking a shower or for not checking in with you when I do. I'm a big girl and I've been on my own for a long time. I shouldn't have to get approval for basic shit."

"You're right. You shouldn't have to, and you don't. I just wanted to know what you were doing so we could make arrangements that you didn't do it alone." He hung his head, picked up a sausage link and took a bite.

That did not sit well with her. "I already said I won't leave the ranch without telling someone, but now I can't do anything alone? What if I want to go for a walk, or hike or whatever you want to call it. Just take off walking across the pasture and into the beyond. Can I do that alone? Do I need to get your permission to get some fresh air?" She closed her mouth and glared at him for a full minute before picking up her coffee and staring off into the distance while she drank it. What was left on her plate no longer held any interest for her. She was so angry. She didn't even want to look at her cousin.

As she continued to drink her coffee, she knew she wasn't being reasonable, but damned if she'd give in. They were only trying to make sure she was safe, she knew that, but if she gave in and took someone with her for every step she made, before long she would feel smothered. She would be desperate to get away from that feeling and would do something stupid just to feel like she wasn't being held back or controlled.

Behind her, she could hear him continuing to eat. She was tempted to pick up her plate, throw it away and go find something to do. Not that she had any idea what. But something, anything away from him, sounded good right now. The only thing stopping her was that she knew she would be back as soon as she finished this cup of coffee for a refill. She didn't want to walk away only to have to come back in ten minutes. She decided to wait until she finished this cup before leaving. That would give her cousin that long to figure out how to get out of the hole he'd dug for himself.

37

Jake checked in with Lurch, making sure there were no last-minute changes to the plans for tonight, a big farewell bonfire. The guys were leaving tomorrow, though the plan wasn't for them to leave early, as they planned on making the same stops on the way back as they'd made on the way up. Not how Jake would have planned the trip if it were up to him. But it wasn't so he kept his mouth shut.

After finishing with Lurch, he went to Malice and Ghost, who were getting ready to make a trip into town for supplies. He made sure their list was right and added a few last minute items after he'd checked the kitchen this morning and see what they were low on, then talked to Kerry, who would take over the overseeing of meals once London was gone, though she wouldn't be cooking most of the time. It had been decided they would keep the prospects cooking, at least for dinner. The rest they'd work out with trial and error.

Now he was finished for a while, he wanted to see Lynnie and maybe get another cup of coffee. It was late enough she was probably up, so he went to the clearing where everyone had been gathering over the last couple of weeks and found that sure enough, she was up, and so was Iceman. They both sat at a table, but she had her back to her cousin, and she looked more than a little pissed off. He took a deep breath, braced himself to play referee between the two of them and approached.

"Who pissed in your cheerios this morning?" he asked as he bent and placed a kiss on top of her head.

Iceman started to say something, but she held up a hand in his direction.

"I don't want to hear from you right now. Give me a minute or ten, then maybe you can talk to me again without eating your teeth." She turned to look at Jake, her eyes narrowed, and he suspected he was about to be tested, the question was, what was going to be tested, his understanding or his patience?

"You and I have already talked about me not leaving the ranch without checking with you, and taking someone with me. But if I wanted to take a walk. Say walk out across the pasture and into the field beyond, maybe where we went riding yesterday, maybe not. What would you say?"

Jake blinked. Was this what she was pissed at Iceman over? Surely it had to be more?

"I'd say go for it. If you want to go farther than within sight of the home site," he circled one finger in the air, indicating the buildings around them, "then I'd ask that you let someone, I'd prefer me, but any of the guys would do, know where you were going and when you planned to be back. I'd be happier if you'd let someone go with you, but I know you're not used to that and might want some solitude. I'd also ask that you take a weapon with you, as protection against any aggressive wildlife or to signal for help should something happen. I don't want to restrict you, Lynnie. I know you're your own person and I respect that, but I do want to make sure you're safe until we can get this reward taken care of."

"Thank you." She gave him a pleased smile before turning to Iceman. "See, I don't need a babysitter all the time. You're the only one who seems to think I'm too stupid to shower on my own."

"I never said that."

She glared back at him.

Jake fought the urge to roll his eyes at the way they bickered like siblings. "Can I trust the two of you not to kill each other while I get some coffee, then we can see what we want to do with the rest of the day."

"I'm good as long as someone's not treating me like a child." Heather turned her back to Iceman and smiled up at Jake.

"We're good. Go get your coffee," Iceman said.

Jake looked back and forth between the two of them for a moment, as if he was unsure he could trust the two of them alone. Then, shaking his head and once he was sure they couldn't see him do it, rolled his eyes, as he went to get coffee. If he was going to have to deal with this kind of bickering, he was going to need the caffeine.

Twenty minutes later, both Iceman and Lynnie were calmer and no longer making threats. Though Jake wasn't sure if it was because of anything he'd done or that they'd both eaten and gotten a little caffeine into their systems. For all he knew it was a combination of both. Not that it mattered. What mattered was they were no longer acting like they were ready to tear each other's heads off.

"So what do we want to do today?" he asked, not for the first time.

"I know I'm hiding, but whatever we decide on, I'd prefer not to leave the ranch," Lynnie said, letting her head hang for a moment. "Give me a day or three to come to terms with a reward on my head, then I'll be ready to face the world again, but I'm just not there yet."

"Hiding for a few days isn't a bad thing." Iceman reached across the table and covered her hand with his. "It gives you time to prepare, to be ready in case there is trouble." He turned his attention to Jake. "I don't care what we do, but I've got to leave this afternoon. I've taken as much time off work as I can for a while, barring an emergency."

"No problem." He thought for a moment. He didn't like how defeated Lynnie looked when she said she was hiding.

How could he help her feel more in control, or at least prepared in case one of the Sons, or someone looking to cash in on that reward, came after her?

"How big's that pistol of yours?" He briefly tightened the arm he'd hooked over her shoulder so she would know he was talking to her.

Lynnie frowned. "It's a .45. Why?"

"Cause I know what we're going to do today." He turned his attention to Iceman. "You have a weapon? And how much ammo do you have with you?"

"I do, but I've only got a box of 9mm rounds with me."

"I'm sure I can find some if we want more. Let's go get some practice in."

"We can do that here?" Lynnie sounded a little hesitant, as if she wanted to go but didn't want to get her hopes up.

"We can. We have a range set up a few miles in. Let me go talk to Lurch, rustle us up some ammo and figure out what vehicle we'll take. You two need to go get your weapons, if you're not already carrying them, plus any ammo or gear you'll want." He knew Lynnie wasn't. She kept hers next to the bed or had since she'd parked the trailer. What he didn't know was whether or not Iceman was carrying, or just had it in his vehicle. Not that it mattered. He checked his watch. "Give me 20 minutes and we'll meet back up here." He waited to get nods from them both before swinging his legs over the bench seat and taking off to get shit done.

38

Heather had been nervous about the trip to the range, or maybe the term makeshift range was a better fit. But thankfully, neither Matt, nor Aaron had treated her like a brainless idiot, which she'd found happened way too often when she went with a guy to the range.

And while the range wasn't a professional setup, she'd been impressed. They had benches at the long-range section for rifles and gong style targets at preset distances. For pistols, they had spinner targets at the preset ranges commonly used for the shorter ranges. Aaron had brought out a package of ringed paper targets and a roll of tape to attach them with.

After he'd gotten targets taped up, Aaron had made sure they all had everything they needed, including ear and eye protection, then they'd lined up and taken their shots.

Heather was focused on what she was doing, lining up the target and maintaining her aim while squeezing the trigger, then lining it back up and starting all over again. She tuned out what the guys were doing, only focusing on her own target, and trying to keep her grouping tight. When she finished her magazine, she relaxed her stance, rolling her shoulders and looking around to find Matt was just finishing his shots and Aaron had dropped the magazine out of his pistol and was in the process of reloading while he waited. She released her clip and set the pistol down on the table in front of her, where she'd set the box of shells Aaron had given her when they'd arrived.

She didn't know where they'd come from, but she'd replace them before she left.

When Matt finished, he popped his magazine free, set both pieces on the table in front of him then looked up at her.

"Are we ready to go check the targets?" Matt asked.

"I am." She turned to Aaron on her other side. "You going too or going to hang back?"

"Let's go."

Aaron picked up a stack of targets and the roll of tape and they each went to the target they'd been using, and pulled down the paper targets. Heather was still looking at hers, all seven shots were in about a five-inch grouping, which she thought was pretty good, when both men brought theirs over to where she stood so they could compare. She looked over at Matt's and saw that he had what looked like twice as many holes in his than she did, not surprising since she was using a smaller pistol that only held seven in the magazine while his was much bigger. His grouping wasn't as tight, without measuring she'd guess maybe an eight-inch spread.

She didn't say anything, just nodded, and turned to look at Aaron's target. His had more holes than hers, but not as many as Matt, making her wonder what the guys were shooting, or at least how many rounds they each held. But his shots were all in a smaller circle than hers.

"You must practice a lot." She nodded toward Aaron's target.

"A bit. Not so much now as I once did."

"Not enough time to shoot as much as you once did?" Matt asked.

Aaron shook his head. "Nah. Not required to spend as much time at the range. When I was in the Army one of the things I did for a while was range duty. Where I had to watch everyone, make sure they weren't being stupid, and no one got hurt."

Matt winced. "Bet that was fun. I've heard a lot of recruits these days have never even touched a gun, much less fired one."

"That's not the term I would have used, but I will say it's not an experience I want to repeat." He tilted his head toward the targets. "We want to put these up on the twenty-five yards targets or stay here on the fifteen?"

"I'm good either way," Heather said, "so I'll leave it up to you two." She folded her target into quarters while she waited for them to decide.

"Actually, how about we move in a bit and go for the seven-yard ones. It will be good practice just in case you end up needing to aim for something closer," Aaron said.

She turned and looked at him, narrowing her eyes as she waited to see if he would actually say what she knew was his motivation. He wanted to see how she handled something closer, because she might have to if someone came after her for the reward.

Could she shoot another human being? She'd thought that very question many times since Daddy taught her to shoot, and since she'd started carrying the pistol in the truck all the time. Mostly it was for emergencies, like an animal that needed to be put down in a hurry, but when she knew men were looking for her, she'd thought about it again.

If it was them or her, knowing what would likely happen to her if she were 'property' of the club Mitch had given her to, she could definitely shoot someone to keep that from happening.

To be sure she could manage to hit whoever came her way, she wanted as much practice as she could get.

They mounted the targets on the seven yard spinners, then went back to the tables where their weapons waited for them. Matt started reloading his magazine, and Heather started to do the same, but Aaron picked up his pistol, and turned to her.

"I noticed how your pistol kicks. I want you try this one," Aaron said holding the pistol flat in one hand, the magazine in the other.

"Are you trying to sell me on another gun?"

He shrugged. "I just want to see how you handle it. You might find you like it better than yours. Or not. Either way it's an experience. And you'll have fun trying something new."

She watched him for the space of two breaths, wondering if he was up to something or she was just suspicious today. Deciding she had nothing to lose she took the pistol, shifted her grip slightly, noticing how well it fit her hand. Better than she'd thought it would given that it was bigger than hers. When she was ready, she took the magazine from Aaron and shoved it into place, then racked the slide to chamber a round. After glancing at both Matt and Aaron to make sure neither had stepped out in front of the firing line, she took aim, flicked the safety off with her thumb and fired at the target.

She didn't say anything as she retrained her sights on the target and fired again. And again. She repeated over and over until the pistol clicked when she squeezed the trigger. She hadn't bothered to count her shots, because she didn't know how many rounds were in it to begin with.

After thumbing the magazine release, she caught it as it fell, and laid both Aaron's pistol and the magazine on the table. Then looked up to find him watching her, a ghost of a smile curling his lips.

"What?" she asked.

His gaze played down her face a moment before returning to hers. "You."

"What about me?" She frowned.

"The way you smile, the way that crease forms between your brows as you concentrate, that look of determination you get when you set your mind to something. All of it."

She blinked, not seeing what he was getting at, then shook her head dismissing it as she turned to look at the target a little over twenty feet away.

"I didn't do too bad. Especially for an unfamiliar weapon."

"Not bad?" Matt said from her other side. "I think you did damn good."

She turned enough to see him, and found his pistol unloaded and laying on the table in front of him. He motioned down range, and together they walked out to the targets. She tilted her head as she tried to decide how she felt about this round. Aaron was right, it wasn't bad for an unfamiliar weapon, but could she do better with her own? She wasn't sure. And she did like that if she had to use it for self-defense, she would have more rounds.

She shook her head, pushing that thought out of her mind as she pulled down the target and replaced it with another. Lost in her own thoughts, she turned and went back to the shooting line, not paying attention to what the guys were doing or even if they were talking to each other. She folded the used target and set it on top of the first one on the bench to dispose of later. She didn't want to leave trash out here for someone else to have to clean up later.

Still lost in her own thoughts, Heather went back to reloading her pistol, even if she wasn't going to shoot it more, it needed to be reloaded.

"All right. You ready for the next round?" Aaron's voice made her look up to find both men had returned, and she hadn't even noticed. If they had been coming to take her back to Alabama, she'd have been in trouble. She needed to get her head out of her ass and pay attention to what was going on around her.

"Sure, what do you have in mind?" She lifted one brow, sure from the glint in his eye that he had something else he wanted her to do.

"Let's do this, I want you to go for both accuracy and speed, but you're not going to aim for just the one target. I want you to switch targets with every shot." Aaron paused.

Heather scowled at him, then looked toward the targets then over at Matt, who watched them, but didn't say anything.

"I can do that. Which pistol do you want me to use?"

"How about you start with yours, we mark those holes, then you do it again with mine?"

"Okay." She finished loading her magazine, glanced at the guys to make sure they were behind the firing line, then loaded the magazine into the pistol and prepared to start shooting. "Do you care what order I do them in or just a different target each shot?"

"Any order you want, but remember you're going for both accuracy and speed."

She started on the left, drew a bead on that target fired, then twisted her body just enough to line up her sights with the center target, then the one on the right. Instead of going back to the one on the left, she went to the center next, then the one on the left. By the time she'd emptied her pistol the targets on either side had been hit twice, but the one in the center had three holes in the paper.

Heather looked from one target to another as they approached, thinking she'd done pretty well. There weren't as many holes to judge the grouping as when she'd been aiming at a single target, but she'd been within three inches of center on every shot.

"How do you plan to mark them?" Matt asked as they approached.

"With this." Aaron pulled a black marker from the back pocket of his jeans and drew a line through each hole on the paper, then went to the next target and did the same. When he was finished with the third target, they walked together back to the firing line. Heather still wasn't sure why they were doing this, but she was enjoying herself, so she decided to just go with it and have fun.

39

J**AKE HANDED HER HIS** pistol. "Try again with this one." He'd reloaded it while she'd taken the shots with her own pistol. Her pistol was nice, but he'd rest easier if she had more than just seven rounds. What if she needed more than that?

She shot well enough that with her pistol she could take out three or even four men if that was what she needed to do, but what if they sent eight or ten? Would she have time to take out that many, even if she had enough rounds?

He watched as Lynnie took aim and moved through the targets the same way she had with her pistol.

"How did that feel?" he asked once she'd emptied the weapon, removed the magazine, and set it on the bench.

"Good. Better than I thought it would."

"In what way?"

She closed her eyes and scrubbed both hands down her face, as if she was trying to clear her mind.

"This is going to sound stupid."

"Don't worry about that. Everyone expresses things differently, tell me why it was better than you anticipated."

"There wasn't as much build up. You know with each shot there's vibrations that echo up your arms and through you. After a while it builds up until you're just done, you can't take it anymore. I expected the build up from this one to be worse, because there are so many more rounds in it, but it wasn't as bad as I thought."

Jake nodded, then tilted his head toward the targets. "Let's go see how you did."

As the three of them made their way downrange to the targets, he wondered what it would take to get her to switch pistols. Even if it was just to start carrying his until they got this threat taken care of.

"Wow," Iceman said, his eyes going wide. "She did even better with your pistol than her own."

Her cousin wasn't saying anything he hadn't noticed himself, and while she'd still been shooting.

They spent another hour or so practicing, burning through the two boxed of ammo he'd brought for each of the pistols, as well as what Iceman had brought for his. Lynnie had shot all three pistols, and had done well with them all.

"Now that you've handled and shot the different pistols, if all things were equal, there was no sentimentality about any of them. Which would you choose to keep?" Jake asked as he started the truck to head back to the ranch house.

"Matt's is too big and too heavy. It doesn't fit my hand well, so it's out. I like my little pistol, but I'm thinking it may be because it's so much like the one Dad gave it to me when I moved out. If I just look at how well they shoot, how they fit in my hand, all that, I'd have to say I liked yours."

He fought the urge to pump his fist in the air like a teenager. This was only a small victory, he still needed to convince her to take it... and carry it. "If your dad gave you one, why did Matt have to give you this one?"

"I don't carry it. I never have," she lifted one shoulder and let it drop, "Its actually at Craig's. I asked him to put it in his safe a while back and never thought about getting it back."

"Have you ever carried?"

"As in a pistol? Not on a regular basis. I might wear my holster to go out shooting or to go into a situation I might need it for venomous snakes, but that's all." She shrugged, her shoulder bumping into his.

"Would you consider it?" he asked.

She was silent, as was Iceman on her other side. He glanced at her, trying to gauge her reaction, and found a crease between her brow, though she wasn't frowning.

"Tell me what you're thinking."

"A lot. I'm not sure if I can put it all into words."

"Can you try? Please?" Jake didn't look at the other man. He wanted to forget he was with them at the moment.

She was staring straight ahead as she opened her mouth, then closed it again. This time she did frown. Then tilted her head and looked at him. She took a deep breath and let it out in a rush.

"I don't know. I have nothing against it, but I'm not sure I can wrap my head around me doing it. Can you give me a few minutes to think about it?"

"I can. I can also give you reasons why I'd ask you to, if you want to hear them."

"Not right now," she said with a shake of her head. "I wasn't expecting this, and I need a little time to get used to the idea."

"Okay," Jake said with a nod. Then, determined to give her the time she'd asked for, he turned his attention to Iceman. "You starting to get hungry? They should have food ready about the time we get back."

"I could eat, then I should start gathering stuff up so I can head out this afternoon."

"You have much to gather?"

"Not really, but I do need to pack up my bedding. I left it open in the back of the truck to get some sunshine and air."

Jake nodded, realizing that Iceman was coming up with things that would keep him busy and give Jake a chance to talk Heather into carrying a weapon. They would both feel better knowing she was armed, just in case. But Jake was going to give her the time she asked for. How long, he wasn't sure, but he could wait until at least after lunch.

40

Heather had known the shooting, the different targets, and different weapons was going somewhere, what she hadn't been prepared for was for Aaron to ask her to carry. Could she? Yeah. Did she want to? Not really. Not all the time, long term at least. But now that she was thinking about it, it made sense. Even the whole different targets with each shot practice that Aaron had asked her to do made sense if she was looking at things from a protection point of view. Who knew how many people would come after her if they wanted the reward? And though she hadn't asked, because she didn't want to know, the reward had to be sizable enough Aaron and Matt thought people would try to take her back to Alabama to collect it.

She still didn't want to think about that. But she had to. It was either that or actually go back and deal with the assholes in Alabama. She didn't want to do that. She wasn't even sure she wanted to go back at all anymore, at least not to stay. Sure, she'd go see her parents, but did she want to live down there? Especially now that she'd seen the beauty up here and found Aaron again?

Was she moving too fast in thinking Aaron wanted her around long term? What they had was good, but he hadn't said anything about anything more long term than getting the jerks from Alabama off her trail. What if that was all he wanted?

Did she want to establish a life up here, only to end up going separate ways then having to see him with someone else?

The truck pulled to a stop, making Heather look up she realized they were back to where they'd started out and Aaron had parked the truck where it had been when they'd gotten into it to go shooting. And she still hadn't decided anything.

On either side of her, both men opened their doors and slid out. She sat for a moment, debating what to do, then mind still unmade she slid out Aaron's side and got out. Why did everything seem so hard? Why couldn't life be easier? She needed a few minutes to herself.

"Is lunch ready?" she asked, still thinking about how to get even a few minutes to herself.

"I don't think so," Jake said after a moment. "I'm not smelling anything, but we can go check, and if you're not ready to eat yet, I'm sure it will hold. Is there something you're wanting to do?"

"I was thinking about a short walk if I have time. I won't go far, and I'll stay on the road."

"Sure, I'll take you," he said.

"No." She set a hand on his chest. "I want a few minutes to myself. I promise I won't go far."

He took a deep breath and met her gaze for a moment.

"Go ahead, I'll see you soon," he said.

The way he kissed her forehead before she walked away sent tendrils of heat swirling through her belly. She enjoyed the way he treated her like she was something special. Like he wanted her around and wanted to make sure she was safe, but he also didn't try to take away her choice. Like he wanted her to want to be there.

Heather found herself smiling to herself as she started down the road that led out to the highway. Her mind drifted to what he'd asked on the drive back from the range. Could she carry a weapon all the time? She could admit to herself that she was torn about the idea.

Not because she didn't think she could use it. If she felt threatened, she had no doubt she would use it. She'd had to use her pistol on snakes before and more than one animal that was suffering and couldn't be saved. Sometimes having to put animals down, or help do it, was part of her job. One that always broke her heart, but she knew she helped far more than she couldn't. And ending suffering was helping too, even if it didn't seem like it at the time.

What had her concerned about carrying all the time was the idea of people who would be scared. People who would confront her and demand to know who she thought she was, a gunslinger from the old west or something? While that would be embarrassing, there was always that one extremist who thought they were hot shit and that no one should be allowed to have a *gasp* gun, and then try to take it away. Those were the ones that worried her.

Maybe she should bring these concerns to Aaron. He knew the area better. He would know if something like that was likely around here.

She looked up and saw a plume of dust approaching. Had someone left earlier and now was on their way back? Was that why lunch wasn't ready when they'd arrived. After Matt had arrived yesterday, she'd heard they had sensors or a camera or something at the front gate and knew when someone came in. Whoever this was must be expected, or they would be ready to stop them. She continued walking, expecting they'd pass her and continue on to the ranch house.

An older model pick up came into view, but it wasn't one she recognized.

She frowned as the truck rolled to a stop a few feet from where she'd stopped to watch it, and driver's window lowered.

"Damn. I never expected you to make it this easy."

"What?" She wanted to ask more but both front doors opened, both men got out. She stepped backwards, wanting to put some distance between them but not wanting to turn her back on them.

"I know someone looking for you, sweetheart, and they're about to make this real worth my while," the driver said as he continued to approach.

She wished now she'd told Aaron yes and that she was carrying one of the pistols. She'd even take Matt's, despite how heavy it had been.

"I'm not going anywhere with you." She stepped back again. But her foot hit a rock, her ankle rolled, and she fell. The last thing she remembered was both men rushing toward her then the world went dark.

41

He didn't like it, but it was just a gut feeling, he had nothing he could articulate better than that. No reason not to tell her to go, enjoy herself. "Go ahead. I'll see you soon." He dropped a gentle kiss against her forehead, then watched as she walked away before turning back to the truck to gather up the trash and dispose of it.

Lynnie had been gone maybe ten minutes when Jake ran into Lurch as he was overseeing getting Tuck and London's things loaded, at least the things they wouldn't need before they left the next day.

"Hey, I was getting ready to send you a message. Where's Iceman?"

"Making sure he's got all his stuff gathered and loaded. He's planning to head back to Dickenson sometime this afternoon, why?"

"Because Watt just called and told me we've got two Kings headed in from the highway. There was a hole in the fence not far from the gate that he noticed while he was checking cattle, so he was mending it and saw them come through the gate. I figured they must be here to see Iceman," Lurch said with a shrug then turned to accept a box from one of the men who was carrying things out. He fit it into place with the rest of the things he was loading into the trailer, stacking and arranging things like a game of Tetris to get as much in the space as he could.

"That's odd, he didn't say anything about expecting anyone." Jake turned away thinking, he didn't think Iceman had anyone coming here. If he had, surely he would have said something to someone, wouldn't he? Especially when Lynnie said she was going for a walk along the road. Maybe he didn't know they were coming. He'd better go check to be sure.

It didn't take him long to locate the visitor, standing in the bed of his pickup, shoving his sleeping bag into the bag it came in.

"Hey, you know why a couple of Kings would be on their way in from the highway?" Jake asked as he stepped up beside the truck and propped both arms on the edge of the bed.

Iceman stopped what he was doing and turned to look at Jake.

"No. Who is it?"

"I don't know. I was just told a couple of Kings. Give me a sec." He pulled out his phone and dialed Watt. Better to go straight to the source for this.

"Hey, those two Kings you saw coming onto the ranch, who were they?"

"The two who were camped out outside the gate last year. The ones who scared London and Kerry by following them."

The hair on the back of Jake's neck stood, telling him something wasn't right. He lifted his gaze to Iceman.

"The men who were here last year following London and Kerry, are they still Kings?"

"No. They were stripped of their colors because of that shit. Well, that and other shit they pulled but no." His eyes went wide. "Are they the ones here?"

"They're not Kings, not anymore. Lock the gate, Watt, and if you can stop them from leaving, do it." He disconnected the call and shoved the phone back in his pocket.

"Go get some of the others." Jake jerked a thumb back toward the bunkhouse, indicating it and the clearing on the other side where several of the brothers had been gathered when he came through a few minutes ago. "I'll go after Lynnie."

"Take the truck. Keys are in it," Iceman said as he vaulted over the side of the truck and took off at a run around the building shouting.

Jake felt like there was band around his chest keeping him from being able to take a breath as he scrambled for the door, climbed in, and started it. As he backed out and turned onto the road a weight settled in his chest that seemed to grow heavier with every foot he travelled.

By the time he'd made the first quarter mile, he knew something was wrong. She hadn't been gone that long. He should have caught up to her, or at least be able to see her, by now. Where was she?

His stomach churned as he pushed the unfamiliar pickup as fast as he dared on the dirt road. Maybe he should have taken the time to grab a vehicle, even one of the dirt bikes, that he was more familiar with, that he knew how it would react when he pushed it.

It took another half a mile for him to catch sight of the pickup in front of him. It was headed the same direction he was, but not moving quite as fast.

He hoped Watt had closed the gate like he'd been told. How far behind him were his brothers?

He wanted to stomp on the gas and just ram them off the road, but there were so many reasons he couldn't. Number one being he didn't know where Lynnie was, or if she'd been secured. The impact might hurt her, and he couldn't stomach the idea. All he could do, at least for now, was to try to catch up with them, and hope Watt could stop them before they got off the ranch.

Checking the rearview again, he hoped to see someone, anyone or more of his brothers coming to help, but so far, nothing. It looked like it was going to be two against two, and they had a hostage.

He didn't know how this would work out, but all he could do was try. He had to get her away from them, to make sure she was safe, then he'd put an end to the threat, for once and for all.

How, though, was still a question. Would a combination of a message sent through these assholes, and another delivered by Hex and his club be enough? Maybe the easiest way would be to pay off the debt her fucker ex has given her to the club to pay them off. But if they were willing to pay that much in reward, how much must the debt be? Jake had built up a bit of a nest egg from both his time in the Army, and since, but he was certain he didn't have the kind of money that would take.

As he continued to close the distance between his borrowed truck and the one he had no doubt Lynnie was inside, he let his mind run freely on things he'd like to do to these two. No matter how much he'd like to make certain they never came back on the ranch, never caused trouble for another member of the Souls or their women, he knew he couldn't. Not in the way he wanted.

Instead, he would have to find a way to make sure they didn't want to come back, but that would have to wait until he made sure Lynnie was safe.

The truck started to slow in front of him, he was catching up faster. He looked past it and saw the gate was closed, and Watt had pulled the ATV he'd been using to fix the fence across the road, adding one more obstacle in case they decided the fence wasn't going to stop them.

If Jake was desperate to get away, neither the gate, nor the ATV would stop him, but from the way they were already slowing, it didn't appear the assholes who had Lynnie we're as crazy as he was. For that he could only be thankful.

Another glance in the rearview showed him a pickup, but it was too far away to do him much good, at least in the moment.

42

HER HEAD HURT. WHY did her head hurt?

Heather tried to lift her hands to find out why her head hurt but couldn't. They wouldn't move. Her mind felt sluggish, slow for some reason she couldn't place. What had happened? Where was she?

Voices she didn't recognize started to filter through her awareness, but she couldn't make out what they were saying. Her head hurt too badly.

She didn't know how much time had passed before she realized her hands were tied. She tried to speak but could tell by the way the voices she couldn't make out never stopped or changed that either she hadn't managed it or what noise she'd managed, though she hadn't heard anything, had made no sense.

Before she could force her mind to work, her entire body moved, she slid backwards, then fell. Now her whole body hurt, and she was no closer to figuring out what was going on.

43

THE TRUCK WAS STILL going way too fast as they approached the gate. Jake watched, helpless, as Watt stepped in front of the ATV and took his time aiming his pistol at the windshield of the oncoming pickup. He slowed as much as he dared, but wanted to get as close as he could, before stopping to confront them.

He wasn't sure how close they were before the driver finally stomped on the brakes, sending the truck sliding to a halt not more than a few feet from where Watt stood, unflinching.

Jake waited as long as he dared then hit the brakes and cranked the wheel, bringing the truck to a sliding stop several feet from the back of the truck he was convinced held Lynnie. As soon as the truck stopped moving, he flung the door open and bailed out. He had the pistol drawn from the small of his back and aimed before he'd rounded the hood.

"Keep your hands where we can see them," he said as he approached, noticing that the men barely glanced at him as they held their hands in clear sight over the dashboard, their attention on Watt in front of them.

He moved close enough it would be hard to miss either one, but not close enough to be hit if they flung open a door then spoke again.

"Get over here Watt and cover them." Jake waited until his brother was within a couple of feet then pinned his gaze on the driver. "Where is she?"

The man moved only one hand, forming a fist with the thumb sticking out, aiming behind him.

"You got them covered?" he asked Watt. He couldn't wait for the truck, and the brothers in it, approaching to make sure she was all right. If she were back there, she should be raising hell. Something wasn't right.

"I got them. Get your girl," Watt said.

Jake shifted his pistol to one hand, and kept it at the ready, in case there was someone else back there waiting to spring a trap, then opened the door, and keeping his body behind it, peeked around the edge and into the truck.

Lynnie lay in the floorboard, all he could see was her feet bound together with duct tape, lying still as death. His heart seized in his chest before his brain got through, telling him if she was dead, they wouldn't have needed to tie her.

He checked the rest of the back seat area and found nothing of concern, then shifted to the other side of the door so he could look in the bed of the truck and make sure there was nothing there. Finding nothing, he holstered his pistol and reached for Lynnie. He grabbed the tape around her ankles and tugged, she slid bonelessly across the floorboard, obviously unconscious.

"What did you do to her?" he demanded.

"All we did was tie her and load her. I swear," the asshole in the passenger seat said.

"She fell and hit her head before either of us laid a hand on her," the driver piped up. "I checked to be sure she was still breathing, then we tied her up and loaded her. She was in the seat until we hit the breaks for this guy." He tilted his head toward Watt.

Not knowing what else to do, he climbed up, braced one knee in the seat and looked down at her as she lay unmoving in the floorboard, her wrists taped together, resting against her chest. His heart ached.

A sound drew his attention, he looked up to find Iceman had opened the rear door across from him.

"Is she alive?"

"Yeah, I'm just trying to decide how to get her out of there without hurting her more." Jake looked back down at her and couldn't help the ache in his chest at how fragile she looked without her usual attitude, nor the spark that usually flashed in her eyes.

"Did they do this?" Iceman asked.

"We only tied her. She fell and hit her head," the driver said again.

"How long's she been out?" Jake asked, still not sure how to get her out.

"Maybe ten minutes," the idiot in the passenger seat piped up.

"I take it you're not alone?" Jake asked Iceman.

"Four others, they've got these guys while we get her out, then they'll handle them."

"Someone needs to take a message back to the Sons that this is done. I don't care what it takes. They come for her again and someone will die. It won't be her." Jake met Iceman's gaze.

The other man nodded.

"I'll make sure they know."

"Let's get her out of here first. Can you brace her head while I drag her out by the feet. Once I've got enough of her out, I'll pick her up and take her back to your truck."

"Sure. Let me get up in there so I can stay with her as you move her, but this might make it easier." He did something Jake didn't see and the seat of the bench in front of him folded up against the back, leaving at least twice as much space.

"That will help." Jake backed out, pressed the seat up and couldn't help but be surprised by the ease with which it folded. Now he could get her out much easier. Iceman was already on his knees in the open space, one hand cupping Lynnie's neck. He looked up and met Jake's gaze.

"She's got a hell of a lump back here, but I don't think there's any blood."

That was good. Still, they needed to get her out of there.

"Ready?" He glanced up at Iceman before returning his gaze to Lynnie's face as he took hold of the tape on her ankles and pulled. Her body slid along the floor without resistance or her moving on her own. That set his teeth on edge. As her hip reached the door jam, he lowered her ankles then scooped her into his arms, one arm under her knees and the other around shoulders. Iceman helped stabilize her head until it hit his shoulder, then Jake eased her out of the doorway and turned for the rear of the truck he'd driven.

By the time he reached the truck, Steele had dropped the tailgate and pulled the sleeping bag that Iceman had been stuffing into its bag earlier and laid it out on top.

"Put her here and let me take a look."

"Why?"

"Former corpsman, man. Let me check her out and see if she needs the ER. I'll take care of your lady." Steele's voice was gentle, yet commanding and matter of fact.

Jake laid her down on the tailgate if nothing else, he needed to get a better look at her and see how badly she was hurt.

"What happened?" Steele asked as he hopped out of the truck. He pulled a knife from his pocket and opened it with a flick of his wrist before handing it to Jake.

"They said she fell and hit her head. They just tied her up after that. Not sure if it's true."

"All right. You take care of the tape I'll look at her head."

Steele was usually pretty quiet, but this take-charge attitude was new. Jake didn't know if he liked it, but was glad someone had an idea what to do and how to check her out.

Doing as he was told, he moved to her feet, carefully cutting the tape, he hated the way there was no resistance to her muscles, her legs moved and flopped as if she was asleep. He wanted more than anything for her to wake up.

"There she is." Steele's voice drew his attention as he peeled the tape from her wrists, trying not to take skin with it.

"She's awake?" he asked.

"She's getting there," Steele said, still cradling her head in his hands as he felt the back of her skull. "She's making faces and reacting to stimuli."

"What does that mean? Do I need to take her into the emergency room?"

"No." The word was slightly slurred as if she wasn't entirely awake, but clear. "No doctor." She grimaced.

Jake's mouth went dry, and his knees almost gave out beneath him as he was able to take his first deep breath since he'd seen her in the floorboard, unmoving. He took her hand and squeezed to let her know he was there.

"Let's see how you bounce back from this before I make any promises, okay?" he said.

"No bouncing, please."

Her brow creased and she tried to turn her face, as if the sun shining down on her hurt her eyes. Jake held a hand up so there was shade across her eyes. The crease eased slightly, but not all the way. He couldn't help but wonder how badly her head hurt.

Steele asked her several questions, looked at her eyes, and made her respond to several commands.

"She's got a lump, but there doesn't seem to be any major damage from what I can see," Steele said. "I recommend you take her in for screening, but I can't force it. However, if there's any nausea, dizziness, or loss of consciousness, she needs to get to the emergency room immediately." He turned and looked down at her again. "Are you sure I can't convince you to in and get checked out?"

She squeezed Jake's hand and shook her head. "No doctor."

"I'll keep an eye out for anything out of place, but especially the things you said. Thanks, man. I don't know what I would have done without someone who knew how to help." Jacke clapped Steele on the back.

"You'd be hauling ass into town for the emergency room, but you're welcome."

44

The pain radiated from the lump she'd felt his firm fingers feeling at the back of her head, but it was better now than before. Still, she hated laying here like an invalid staring up at the sky.

"Can I sit up?" She squinted as much from the bright light as from the pain.

"Slowly. Make sure you're not dizzy or nauseated," the man she thought was named Sterling or Silver, something metallic, no, those weren't right, but it hurt too much to think about it right now, said.

A hand cradled her neck and helped her sit up, she sat for a moment, blinking. It was easier to open her eyes without the sun shining down into them.

"How are you feeling?" Aaron asked. It was his hand on her neck, and still holding one of hers.

"My head hurts, but I don't feel sick."

"Good, sit like that for a minute and give yourself a minute. If you're still good then, we'll let you move a little more," the metal man said.

She looked around, wondering where they were and how long she'd been out. It didn't take her long to realize they were still on the ranch, if only barely.

"What are they going to do to them?" She nodded to where several men had the guys who had stopped her on the road out of the truck and stood in a semi-circle trapping them against the truck.

"That depends. Tell me what you remember."

"I was walking, like I told you, when I saw the truck coming up the road. I stopped and stepped out of the road, expecting them to pass by so I could continue. But they stopped. Said I made it too easy for them. I was backing away as they came closer when I slipped. Falling is the last thing I remember." She blinked several times at Aaron, wondering how he'd known so quickly that something was wrong, but didn't want to ask, not now.

After several breaths she braced her hands on both sides of her hips and used them as leverage to twist, swinging her legs off the tailgate.

"Hey, what's up?" Aaron asked.

"I'm getting ready to move."

"Steele said to take it slowly," he said.

She looked up and saw the crease between his brows, his worry for her touched her heart. And Steele. That was metal man's name.

She frowned and glanced around. "I am taking it slow. I'm just putting my feet down. Where has he gone?"

"He went to see if the others need any help."

She glanced in that direction but turned back to Aaron after just a moment. She was curious but couldn't gather enough will to care overmuch. Heather let her head hang as she took several deep breaths. She just wanted this over with. Wanted to get on with her life. What would it take to make this all stop? Did she need to go back to Alabama so people would stop following her, stop looking for her? The idea made her stomach churn. Leaving Aaron was the last thing she wanted to do, but she hated bringing trouble to his doorstep.

That thought alone told her she wasn't thinking clearly. Now wasn't the time to make any long-term decisions. Especially not anything rash like turning herself over to a motorcycle club that had driven her to flee more than a thousand miles to begin with.

"Can I get down yet?"

"How's your head?"

"Painful but I'm not dizzy."

"All right. Then let's try it." Aaron's hands were gentle as he cupped either side of her waist and helped her slide off the tailgate. "Don't try to go anywhere yet. Just stand still and get your bearings."

Pain shot through her entire body as her feet hit the ground, but she bit back the groan that fought to escape. She could do this. It would pass, a deep breath helped, then another. After what seemed like only a few seconds, but was likely a minute or longer, she tilted her head back to look up at Aaron.

"Ready to move?" he asked.

"Yeah, where are we going?"

"We're going to go around and get in the truck. You good with that?"

"Yeah." All she wanted was to get back to the ranch, to her trailer, maybe even to her bed where she could stretch out, hopefully with him next to her and rest until her head quit hurting. Maybe take something and see if that would help.

She started slowly, then after the first steps didn't make her head hurt any worse, she moved faster. It didn't take long before she was sitting in the passenger seat, door closed and waiting for Aaron to go around to the other side.

"This isn't your truck," she said when he climbed up into the seat.

"No, it's Iceman's. He told me to take it while he got the others when we realized something was wrong." He started the engine, then had to maneuver it back and forth a couple of times before they were turned around and headed back to the main ranch.

Something needed to be done to make this stop but she didn't know what and she didn't know how. She'd have to think more about it later, because her head hurt too much to think it through now.

45

Jake took Lynnie back to the main ranch, gave her the Tylenol Steele recommended and got her tucked into bed. He'd been hesitant to let her sleep, but Steele had assured him it was the best way for her to heal, but that she'd need to be woken and checked on regularly. He could do that. Hell, he doubted he'd be able to get very far from her for a while.

"Stay with me." Lynnie reached for him as he went to turn out the light and let her rest.

"Are you sure?"

"I want you here. I want to feel you hold me."

How could he deny a request like that? He kicked off his boots and climbed up onto the bed behind her, careful not to jostle her too much as he pulled her into his arms.

He lay still, holding her and reveling in the feel of her there, safe, as he puzzled out how to put an end to this threat. Her breathing evened out and she fell asleep in the first fifteen minutes, but he lay there another thirty, making sure she wasn't restless, and considering how best to solve his problem.

When he got up, he eased off the bed, grabbed his boots and tiptoed from the room, so he didn't wake her. In the front room he sent a few messages and put his boots back on. He wouldn't go more than a few steps away from the trailer in case she called out, he wanted to hear her. He also needed to talk to his brothers and make a few calls and the last thing he needed was for her to wake up and overhear him.

He sent several texts, pacing the living room the whole time, as he got things lined up as best he could this way. Everything else needed to be handled either in person or at least with a call. When the time came to step outside, he checked the time and found he'd been up less than an hour. He'd let her sleep a little longer before waking her, but he did peek into the bedroom and make sure she was okay and sleeping peacefully, then slipped outside as quietly as he could.

Jake hadn't taken five steps from the door of the trailer before Iceman stood in front of him, his brow creased with concern.

"How is she?"

"She's okay. She's sleeping right now."

"Is that safe? I always heard you keep someone awake after a blow to the head."

"I heard that too, but Steele said it's safe to let her sleep. We will need to wake her every couple of hours to make sure she's still okay, but right now we just let her sleep."

"All right, but I want to see her when you wake her."

"She needs to be woken in about an hour. You can do that." He glanced at the trailer, as if he could see through it to her, and made a decision. One that would solve at least one of his problems, for now. "What time do you need get out of here to make it to work?"

Iceman shook his head. "I'm not going home. I already called in. I'll stay another day, make sure everything is good here."

"You sure? She wouldn't want you to get in trouble at work."

"I'm sure. Besides, my president is my boss. He understands about family and that we have some things to make up to your club. On top of that, he let me know that it's his fault these asshats found her. He's feeling guilty and will likely let me have whatever time I want."

"I won't say I don't appreciate it. I do. But it wasn't necessary. We've got a lot of people around here. Tell me more about how those idiots finding her is his fault?"

"It seems he and some of the others were sitting around the shop one evening after hours and shooting shit. Someone asked where I'd gotten off to and he told them. What he didn't know was that Rooster was hanging around, trying to find dirt on the Kings. He'd heard about the bounty on her head and that her ex had remembered she had a cousin up this way. He put two and two together, leading them here. As for your people, half of them are leaving tomorrow. There's a lot going on here and that's no one's fault, but I can help. If I need to, I can stay longer. Cowboy will understand."

"Thanks. She's on the bed, but go on in if you want. I'll feel better if you're keeping an eye on her, in case she needs anything while I make some phone calls. I'm going to put an end to this reward bullshit today."

"I didn't know you had the pull to do that."

"I've got a couple of connections and I've been working on it, but it's not going fast enough. I'm going to make promises and owe a few favors, but I don't want this to happen again, no matter what I have to do." Jake tilted the top of his head toward where Lynnie lay in bed, sleeping.

"I'll make sure nothing happens to her," Iceman said.

Jake nodded, leaving his woman's cousin to make sure she was safe. His woman? Since when had he started thinking of her as his? His mind spun as Iceman stepped past him and into the trailer. As much as he might want to, he didn't have time for this. Thinking about what she meant to him was a pleasure he didn't have time to take, not as long as men were looking to cash in on capturing her and taking her back to Alabama and the Sons for the reward money.

Jake pulled up Hex's number on his phone and pressed dial. The phone rang in his hear and he thought about how best to address this. In the end, all that mattered was the result. He didn't care what it cost him.

"Hey, I didn't expect to hear from you so soon. I haven't found out anything new."

"That's okay. I have. I need something and I don't care what it costs. Money now, a favor in the future. Whatever, it's yours." Jake glanced around to make sure there was no one near and he wasn't overheard.

"If it's in my power, it's yours. You know that," Hex said. "Tell me what you need."

Jake relayed what had happened here this afternoon, then continued with what he needed done. "Find Mitch Coleman and deliver him to the Sons. Tell them that this is the person who incurred the debt and the person who will be paying it. Heather is off the table, permanently. They are to remove the reward for her immediately, and if she has any more trouble stemming from this little stunt of theirs, then they won't have to worry about it for long because they will no longer be breathing, and their bodies will never be found."

"Okay, I don't have any problem with that, and I'll gather a couple of men who won't mind helping. We've been working on putting an end to the Sons for a while. We are close to having what we need. Then you won't have to worry about them anymore anyway. Any requests for what kind of condition Coleman is in when we deliver him?"

Jake blinked. He hadn't thought about that. He'd been too concerned with getting it done. "Let's go with the same condition they put on the reward. No permanent injuries."

"Sounds good to me. You know where to find him?"

"Not a clue." Jake wished he had more, because that would make this whole operation faster, but he'd have to deal with it. Hex would be able to find him, it was just a matter of how quickly. "Let me know once it's done. Not that I'll drop my guard any time soon, even once the message has been delivered, but it will be good to know."

"No worries. I'll stay in touch. And not just about this. I'm sure you'll hear from me soon," Hex said.

"I'll look forward to it. Let me know if you need anything from me. In the meantime, I'm going to see what I can do to make sure we're covered in case someone else shows up before the word gets out that the reward is cancelled."

"Take care, I'll be in touch." Hex disconnected the call.

Jake went in search of Lurch, he needed to find out what they'd done with the assholes after he'd left and figure out what they had to do to make sure everyone here stayed safe. The last thing they needed was for any of the women to get in the middle of something like this. They didn't want any of them hurt, and he needed to do his share to make sure they were doing everything they could.

46

"Heather, I need you to wake up."

Heather turned her head away. She didn't want to wake up. Her head hurt. Come to think of it, most of her body ached, but not as bad as her head.

"I know you want to sleep, but you can't. I need you to talk to me for a minute. Then you can sleep more if you want."

She knew the voice but couldn't place it, not at the moment. And she didn't want to wake up. She wanted to lie here being held. But wait, she wasn't being held. Aaron was gone. That more than the voice pulled her to open her eyes.

"What is it? Where is Aaron?" she asked as she rolled toward the voice and opened her eyes.

Matt stood beside the bed, a crease of concern between his brows. "Answer a couple of questions for me and I'll let you go back to sleep. What day is today?"

"Tuesday, why? And aren't you leaving so you can go to work tomorrow?"

He shook his head. "Not yet. I took tomorrow off. I can't leave right now."

She frowned. "Why not? I don't want you putting your job at risk because of me."

"I will do what I need to do, and Cowboy won't fire me over this." He waved one hand, as if dismissing the issue. "What's my full name?"

"Matthew James Fields, why are you asking me that?" Heather pushed herself up, so she sat in the middle of the bed, glaring at him.

"Do you remember what happened this morning?"

She couldn't help looking at him like he'd lost his mind. "The target shooting, or the idiots who scared me into falling when they thought they'd try to collect on the reward those friends of Mitch's put out?"

The concerned crease on Matt's forehead eased.

"You still haven't answered me." She scooted to the edge of the bed and swung her legs off, waiting long enough for him to step back and out of her way before standing.

Her head throbbed at the movement, and she paused. Matt reached for her, taking her arm as if she was unsteady. She stared at his hand for a moment then remembered someone telling her and Aaron that if she was dizzy then she needed to go to the emergency room. Was she dizzy? She blinked a couple of times, thinking about it. No. Not dizzy, nor was she nauseated, she just hurt.

"I'm okay. I'm not dizzy. I just need to pee."

"Are you sure?"

She sent him a scowl to let him know what she thought of his second guessing what she'd told him, then turned and made her way into the trailer bathroom.

When she'd finished her business, she went to the sink to wash her hands and couldn't hold back the squeak of surprise that escaped as she caught her own reflection.

"What's wrong? Are you all right? Did you fall?"

She twisted around and opened the door, not bothering to disguise her irritation with him. "Did it sound like I fell? You would have heard since you're hovering right outside the door like some kind of creeper." She turned back to the mirror and frowned again. "Why didn't you tell me I look like shit?"

Her hair had come loose from her ponytail and now stood on end, making her look like a crazed person. And that was before even considering the dirt and grime streaking her face.

"I was more worried about how you're doing, you know your health, than what you look like, or how your hair's done." Snark fairly dripped off Matt's voice.

She didn't even look at him as she dug out a washcloth, wet it and started cleaning her face. Oh my god. Aaron had seen her like this too and hadn't said a word.

Her face heated at the idea, but she did her best to hide it as she scrubbed at the dirt, doing her best to get it all, but suspecting she'd need a shower as she felt bits of dirt and rocks in her hair as she tried to smooth it back into place.

She glanced over at Matt who stood watching her, concern clear on his face.

"Will you do me a favor?"

"What?"

"Will you go see if there's anyone around in the bunkhouse, and if the showers are open?"

"You can shower in here you know."

"I know, but there's more room in there. And then there's the hot water too. I haven't figured out the water heater on this."

Matt rolled his eyes but turned toward the door. "I'll be right back, and I'll show you the water heater again before I go." He said more but she suspected he was muttering to himself because she couldn't make it out.

She gathered her towels, clean clothes, and her shower bag, when he came back to tell her the bunkhouse was empty, she was ready.

"Are you sure you're up for this?" Matt asked as he walked with her into the bunkhouse.

Heather didn't bother to respond, instead sending him a scathing glare that said more clearly than words that she was tired of him asking and to shut the hell up. Thankfully, he didn't say anything more as they went inside, and she disappeared into the bathroom.

47

Jake stepped into the bunkhouse, intending to snag a couple of sandwiches out of the refrigerator and take them to the trailer so there was food available when Lynnie got hungry. What he didn't expect was to find Iceman sitting on the sofa, flipping through channels on the TV, when he walked in.

"I thought you were keeping an eye on Lynnie?" Jake said, fighting the urge to race out and make sure she was okay.

"I though you'd figured out by now that woman has a mind of her own," her cousin shot right back. "I woke her to check on her a bit ago, she decided to use the bathroom and saw herself in the mirror, then decided she had to have a shower." He waved one hand toward the door that led to the bathroom and communal shower across the room.

Jake looked at the door, then back to Iceman then turned and went into the bathroom.

"You in here, baby?" he called as he stepped in the door. He could hear water running and assumed she was in the shower. He didn't want to startle her and have her slip and fall.

"Aaron?"

"Do you think Iceman would let anyone else in here while you're showering?" He stepped farther into the room and saw her standing under the spray from the center showerhead. She stood facing him, water hitting her back. Her hands were buried in her hair, bubbles over most of her head. She grinned as he stopped and stared, unable to help himself.

"I'm shocked he let you in here." She waggled her eyebrows at him before turning around and tilting her face up to the shower head.

Jake let his gaze play down her body, taking in every curve and making note of several bruises marring her skin, and wishing he could give those asshole's matching ones for every single one she wore, but they were already gone, and he couldn't. Knowing that Hex would make sure Mitch paid in pain for what he'd done to her helped, but he didn't know if it was enough. He didn't know if it would ever be enough.

"Was your point in all this just to tease me?" he asked even though she had her back to him and her face under the spray. He couldn't help but watch the way she moved, the way she wiggled her ass, he was sure without any idea what it did to him. He stayed on the far end of the bathroom, fighting the urge to step into the shower with her. To pull her close and hold her, reassure himself she was there, and she was okay.

"I had no clue you'd come in and interrupt my shower, so how could my point have been to tease you?" she said as she reached for a bottle she'd set nearby dumped some in her hand then worked it through her hair.

"Then why the mid-day shower?"

She twisted around and gave him a look that said without words that she thought he was being stupid.

"I was filthy. I had dirt and rocks in my hair, not to mention smeared all over my face. I can't believe you put me in bed like that."

"I was more worried about making sure you were okay than that you were clean. I'm glad to see you're feeling well enough to give me shit, though. How's your head?" He wanted to ask more but knew her well enough to know she would only put up with so much hovering and he didn't want her pissed at him. Not too soon.

"It hurts, but not as bad as before."

"I was getting ready to bring you something to eat. Does anything sound good?"

She turned around to face him, worked her shoulders as if flexing so the water hit different spots as she narrowed her eyes at him.

"I think you're lingering so you can watch me."

He wasn't going to admit it, at least not so easily. But was there anything wrong with that? It wasn't like he hadn't slept in her bed last night, and the night before. And would be again tonight. And for as long as he could foresee if he had his way.

"Would you have a problem with it if I was?"

He watched as she pursed her lips and rolled her eyes to one side, as if considering it. Jake had to put his hands in his pockets to keep from reaching for her, even so far away.

"No, I don't think I would. And you're so far away." She shot him a mischievous grin before turning back to the spray to rinse her hair again.

Jake found himself unable to leave, or even look away. She had captured more than his attention, he knew that a long time ago, but after what happened today, he knew he needed to tell her, to make sure she knew.

"Will you hand me my towel?" She turned off the water with one hand, holding the other toward where she'd set her folded towel on the edge of the sink several feet away.

"Since you asked so nice." He snagged the towel as he advanced on her, unfolding it with a flick of his wrist. He gently wrapped it around her, then carefully blotted her dry, including working as much moisture from her hair as he could while still being careful of her bruises and the knot on the back of her head. When he was finished, he wrapped it around her torso and used it to tug her close. "Stay with me." He looked down into her face, watching her every expression as he prepared to lay himself bare for her.

"I'm already staying here."

"Yeah, but that's temporary. I mean make it permanent. I want you here. I didn't plan on it, but I've fallen for you, hard."

She smiled at him. "You're not the only one. But what about the people looking for me? I can't bring that kind of danger to the people here. They weren't looking for the kind of trouble following me."

"I'm working on that. Give me another couple of days and it should be gone. Please," Jake never thought he'd hear himself beg, not for something like this, "say you'll give us a chance."

Lynnie stared up at him for what seemed like a decade before nodding. "I'll give it a chance, but I can't make any promises if something like this happens again. I like Kerry, Donna, and the others too much to put them at risk."

"It won't come down to that." He didn't know quite how, not yet, but he would make sure it didn't.

"Good, then kiss me." She stretched up, pressing her nearly naked body against him as she wrapped her arms around his neck and tugged him down for a searing kiss.

He lost himself in her touch, her taste, and thanked everything holy that the assholes today hadn't made it off the ranch with her or hurt her worse than a few bruises and a headache.

His phone ringing from his pocket pulled him back to the present. He pulled away from Lynnie gave her ass a squeeze as he pulled out his phone. The call was Hex.

"I need to take this. Your cousin is out there so put on clothes before you come out." He tilted his head toward the door, reluctantly released her, and headed for it, answering the call as he went. "Talk to me."

"It's done."

"What is?" He wanted to look back at Lynnie and make sure she was all right, but he knew she was and just wanted another glimpse of her. Instead he continued into the bunkhouse, listening to his old friend as he went.

"The ex has been delivered to the Sons. They understand that they will not be getting your girl, and if they don't retract the reward, effective immediately, then they'll be at war with not just the Warriors but the Souls as well. Since they have no idea our reach, they've decided it would be in their best interest to write off the debt, or at least whatever portion of it they can't collect from the piece of shit that incurred it."

"Great. I owe you one," Jake said, knowing it wouldn't be as immediate as it seemed, but it would work out in the end.

"I'll remember, but it seems I owed you one already."

"Not in my estimation. That was duty. I did my job. This was a favor."

"You saved my life. That's not duty. But I'm glad I could do this for you."

They talked a couple of minutes longer before ringing off. Jake pocketed his phone as he leaned back against the kitchen sink and took a deep breath.

"Was that what I think it was?" Iceman's question reminded him he wasn't alone. Not that it mattered, nothing had been said that would get him into trouble.

"The Sons say they are retracting the reward. It may take a few days for word to get out, but the threat will be over soon."

"Good. I'll let you know when the Kings get word." He pulled out his phone and sent a text before looking back up at Jake. "I'm still staying tonight, but then I'll head back. I feel better about leaving now that I know that's taken care of. Do I want to know what it took?"

"I had a friend in Mobile have a talk with her ex and another with the Sons." Jake lifted one shoulder and let it fall. "By the way, you interested in selling that trailer?"

Epilogue

Two weeks later

Heather placed a hand in the small of her back and stretched. As much as her back ached, she was glad to be doing something again. Today had been her second day at her new employer, the vet Lurch had told her they used at the ranch, and so far, she liked Dr. Kurt, as well as the rest of the staff.

After making sure everything had been taken care of, and checking in with the nigh tech, who's name she couldn't recall at the moment, she grabbed her coat and headed out. She was tired, but it was a good tired. As she made the twenty-minute drive back to the ranch, she couldn't help but be glad she wouldn't have to worry about dinner. Either they would join the rest of the hands and have whatever was being served, or Aaron would fix them something. She was good either way, as long as she didn't have to do it herself.

Thinking of Aaron, she smiled to herself at how he'd taken care of her, and worried over every little thing. Yes, it was irritating sometimes, but also endearing. It told her he cared. He also didn't seem to care that she couldn't get in the habit of calling him Jake like everyone else did. The one time she'd brought it up, he'd said he liked her calling him Aaron, it was their thing, so she'd quit trying.

Heather pulled up outside her borrowed trailer and sat for a minute, wishing for the first time since she'd arrived here, that she had either an apartment or a house. If only so she had room for a proper bathtub. Because right now, nothing sounded better than a soak in a tub of steaming water to ease her sore muscles.

The truck door beside her opened, startling her. She couldn't help the way she jumped or the high-pitched squeak that escaped.

"Sorry, babe, I didn't mean to scare you. I saw you pull in, but not get out and I got worried." Aaron wrapped one arm around her and tugged her into his embrace. "Is everything okay?"

"Yeah, I'm just tired and was wishing on stars." She tipped her head back and kissed him, losing herself for a moment in his taste, then pulling away. "How long do I have before dinner?"

He checked his watch. "About half an hour, why?"

"I'm in desperate need of a hot shower." She wrinkled her nose as she thought of the things she'd gotten on her today at work. "Can I talk you into clearing the bathroom for me?"

Matt had shown her how to use the hot water in the trailer, but that tank was tiny, and she wanted more than it gave her in hot water.

He watched her for a moment then nodded. "Sure. Want time to yourself or you want me to come talk to you while you shower?"

"I wouldn't say no to talking, but you're keeping your clothes on this time. I'm hungry and have no intention of missing dinner again."

"But it was fun," Aaron said with a laugh as he stepped back and gave her space.

She climbed down from the truck and shot him a grin as he headed for the door, and she went into the trailer. "I'll be right there."

By the time she went into the bunkhouse, there were a couple of Aaron's brothers in the common room of the bunkhouse, but the bathroom and showers were empty. She waved as she ducked inside, eager to get clean. She'd stripped out of her dirty clothes and turned on the water and was waiting for it to warm up when Aaron came in.

"How was your day?"

"Good. We were busy, so the day went quickly."

"And you got dirty."

"Babe, I'm a vet tech. I get dirty every day."

"So this shower as soon as you get home is going to be a regular thing?"

"Yeah, probably," she said, stepping under the spray.

"I can deal with that. If you'll let me know when you leave, I can make sure it's available when you get home."

That was sweet. And just another of the many reasons she loved him.

"I'll do that. Tell me about your day."

"Ranch work mostly, but I did get a couple of interesting calls."

"Oh?" She poured shampoo into her hand, then worked it into her hair, biting back a groan at how good it felt to work her fingers along her scalp.

"First was a call from Cowboy telling me he'd heard through the grapevine that the Wandering Sons had been raided. Word went out on the grapevine that any and all offers slash contracts they'd put out might as well be void because they were no longer in a place to honor them."

Heather froze for a moment, then used her arm to wipe soap suds from her face.

"Does that mean what I think it means?"

"It does if you think it means that having to look over your shoulder for someone out for the reward is over, for good."

"Are you sure?"

"As sure as I can be. I heard the same news from the Tucson chapter, and I called Hex to be sure."

She rinsed her hair and applied the conditioner, moving on auto pilot as she processed the news.

"I could go back if I wanted," she said, not sure she could believe it.

"You could." He fell quiet while she rinsed her hair and body. When she shut off the water, he stepped in with her towel, gently blotting her dry, a habit they'd gotten into over the last couple of weeks. He didn't always join her in the shower or in the bathroom, but when he did, he didn't let her dry herself, but took care of her. "Do you want to go back?"

Heather turned and looked at him, searching his face for any sign of what he wanted. But she saw nothing. He'd carefully schooled his expression to blankness.

"No." The words came out as barely more than a breath. She watched his face a moment longer. "Not unless you do too. I don't care where I am, as long as you're there too."

"Thank God." Aaron lowered his head and covered her mouth in a searing kiss that stole all thoughts of being anywhere but here, from her mind. All that mattered was the two of them, here and now. "I have something I need to ask but wanted to make sure you wanted to be with me first."

"What?" She frowned at him.

"Marry me. I want you to stay forever. I'm trying to convince your cousin to sell me the trailer, or I'll pick up another somewhere else, but I don't ever want you to leave. I want you with me always. I can't imagine anyone else I want to ride through life with." He wrapped his arms around her and held her against him as he gazed down at her.

Her heart thundered in her ears. Had he really just asked her for forever? To be a permanent part of her life? She'd hoped for this, but hadn't dared think he might want the same thing.

"There's nowhere I'd rather be. As stupid as it sounds, I'm glad Mitch turned out to be as stupid as he did."

Aaron growled.

"I know you don't like me talking about him and I won't even disagree that he got what was coming to him. But if he hadn't done what he did, I never would have come north and found you again. And I'd go through a lot more than I did to have what I have now."

"You still haven't answered me."

"I did, but not in the way you wanted." She smiled and lifted one hand to cup his face. "Yes, I'll stay with you. I'll take your growly moods and cranky scowls, because you're the best thing that ever happened to me. I'm not going to walk away from that, ever." She stretched up and placed a peck of a kiss on the end of his chin. Her stomach rumbled, reminding her she'd missed lunch. "Now I'm hungry, so let me get dressed. After we eat, I'll let you drag me to bed so we can celebrate."

"Put your clothes on, woman. I'm making plans for that celebration already."

Heather shook her head and smiled to herself as she pulled on her clothes and combed out her hair. She never would have guessed things would end up this way as she'd fled Alabama, but she wouldn't trade a single moment with Aaron for anything. This was where she was meant to be and where she intended to stay.